'Be my mistress. I will pay you well and you will no longer have to endure my mother's slights.'

Mary Margaret dropped the cup of tea she had just lifted to her lips. It hit the table with a thump, sending scalding liquid all over the cloth. Neither one paid it any mind.

'You jest, and very cruelly,' she said.

Amazed at his bluntness, Ravensford shook his head slowly. 'No, I don't believe I do, Miss O'Brien.'

He downed the whiskey, wondering if it would numb his nether parts. He could only try, for it was obvious she was not going to help him in that area.

She stormed to her feet. 'I am not…not a loose woman. I might not be your equal, my lord, but that does not make me someone you can take advantage of.'

He stood, admiring the way fury put colour into her high cheeks and brought a flutter to her breasts. How he wanted her.

'My apologies, Miss O'Brien. It was my baser self speaking.' He gave her a roguish grin. 'But should you change your mind, don't hesitate to tell me.'

Georgina Devon began writing fiction in 1985 and has never looked back. Alongside her prolific writing career, she has led an interesting life. Her father was in the United States Air Force, and after Georgina received her BA in Social Sciences, from California State College, she followed her father's footsteps and joined the USAF. She met her husband, Martin, an A10 fighter pilot, while she was serving as an aircraft maintenance officer. Georgina, her husband and their young daughter now live in Tucson, Arizona, USA.

Recent titles by the same author:

THE RAKE

*Look out for Perth's story,
coming in 2002!*

THE REBEL

Georgina Devon

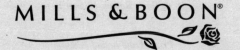

MILLS & BOON®

MILLS & BOON and MILLS & BOON with the Rose Device are registered trademarks of the publisher.

First published in Great Britain 2001
Harlequin Mills & Boon Limited,
Eton House, 18-24 Paradise Road, Richmond, Surrey TW9 1SR

© Alison J. Hentges 2001

ISBN 0 263 82745 3

Set in Times Roman 10½ on 13 pt.
04-0901-58104

Printed and bound in Spain
by Litografia Rosés S.A., Barcelona

Chapter One

Andrew Dominic Wentworth, Earl of Ravensford, paused in the act of bringing a glass of Irish whiskey to his mouth. The door to the library where he lounged had opened with a vengeance and then slammed shut. The delicate scent of lavender filled the room.

'I am tired of dancing to your tune,' a husky female voice stated.

A smile tugged at Ravensford's lips. A wife or mistress. In his experience, they were the only women who occasionally danced to a man's tune, and then only for something in return. Mothers and sisters did whatever they wanted regardless of what they were told or what was involved.

'You will do exactly as I tell you,' a man's light tenor replied.

A low, feminine growl followed the arrogantly

superior words. 'What if I don't? What if I tell you no?'

The man chuckled low in his throat. 'Then I will be forced to do something you won't like, and we both know what that is.'

The woman groaned, her husky voice ending in a sob. 'What do you want?'

She sounded completely defeated. The man must have a powerful hold over her. For some strange reason, Ravensford felt disappointment. He had wanted her to win their contest.

'That is more like the dutiful miss I know you to be.' Sarcasm and gloating filled each word.

'Only because you have something I value highly.' The woman's rich, nerve-tingling voice caught on the last word.

Her voice was incredible. The deep, almost growling tone demanded attention at the same time as it created an image of a sleek feline. Ravensford found himself entranced. Never had a sound aroused him so, not even his former mistress's voice when she was in the throes of passion.

He was a connoisseur of women, often finding himself embroiled with a second before he was free of the first. Why hadn't he seen this woman—or heard her? For if he had, he would have remembered her voice. He had never heard one so sensual and arousing. Just sitting here listening to her made him want to experience her in other ways.

With very little enticement he could be enthralled. He imagined the woman to be small and supple like the cat her low, raspy tone brought to his mind. For a brief instant he wondered if she would purr like a contented feline when a man stroked her. It was an errant thought and one he had no business thinking where a respectable woman was concerned. And respectable she must be or she would not be in his mother's establishment.

The Countess was fanatical about other people's morals, an unusual trait in someone of her generation. More often than not, he had found others of his mother's age to be more risqué than most people closer to his age.

However, it was time he made his presence known. He took another sip of the liquor and started to rise.

'I want you to stay close to the old Countess. I have need of some of her possessions.' The last word was said with a repulsive snicker.

Ravensford decided not to stand. Something was afoot. Something unsavory from the man's words, and something that involved his mother.

'Haven't I been doing exactly that?' Exasperation and perhaps remorse tinged every word the woman spoke.

Ravensford's curiosity increased. The urge to reveal his presence was strong, but he resisted. It was his experience that when one avenue was cut off a person would find another. Words were not enough for him to have the couple arrested. Nor did he want to. The woman was reluctant and he found himself unwilling to harm her when he did not even know her. His best course was to tell his mother that someone in her household intended to rob her, even though he doubted it would do any good.

As for him confronting the two now, that would not do either. He had no evidence but their words and, even with his rank, he could do nothing without more substantial evidence. Nor would he want to. He had spent his life championing those not as fortunate as himself. The game laws, Corn Laws, all of those were biased for the wealthy. As were the criminal laws. No, he would not do anything until he actually caught the pair in the act of stealing.

He had arrived at his mother's Irish estate early this morning. Derry House and the surrounding farms had been part of her dower, and she returned to them on a regular basis. This time, she had summoned him to attend her. Never a good omen.

'You have been a good little girl so far,' the man said, focussing Ravensford's thoughts back on the couple. 'See that you remain such.' His light tenor was at odds with his implied threat. 'Best you go before someone notices us.'

There was a sharp inhalation. 'Until you command my presence again,' the woman finished bitterly.

She definitely did not like dancing to the man's tune. Ravensford wondered if she disliked the job or the man or both. And what was his hold over her?

The sound of footsteps followed by the opening and closing of the door told Ravensford he was alone once more. The large centre log in the fireplace cracked and split, sending sparks scattering through the room. The servant who had started the fire had forgotten to put the screen in front. He rose and stomped out any little flames before they could do damage to the Aubusson rug.

While the thought of someone stealing from his mother was unpleasant, he found himself intrigued by the turn of events. Perhaps a dull, but comfortable and mandatory visit to his parent would become an entertaining proposition.

If nothing else, he had a mystery to occupy his mind. He did not recognise the man's voice and was not sure he would notice if he were to hear it again in ordinary circumstances, for it was not re-markable. The woman was another story. He would remember her deep-throated purr in his dreams. Whatever she did in his mother's house-hold, he would soon find out. Then the game would begin.

A wry grin twisted his well-shaped lips. With the luck he had been having lately, she would be a drab tabby and married.

He finished the whiskey and strode from the room. Action was always preferable to inactivity. It was a maxim he had put to frequent good use in the House of Lords. He was sure it would be so here.

Ravensford propped one Hessian-shod foot on his knee, careful not to rub dirt on his beige pan-taloons. He was as casual in his dress as his mother was meticulous, but casual did not mean dirty. Then there was his valet, who would make him miserable for several long minutes if he returned messed up after so short an absence.

Across a small space, his mother reclined on a gold-lined chaise-lounge, looking frail to the point of ethereal. Her silver hair was cut fashionably short, an ideal foil for the oval perfection of her creamy complexion. She was a handsome woman and had been the toast of the *ton* in her first Season. A pale lavender afternoon dress, trimmed lavishly with Brussels lace, accentuated the slim curves of a young girl. All in all, she was very well preserved.

Ravensford wished her mind were as tidy as her person. She was, to put it generously, scatter-brained. He did not relish the task of telling her about the proposed robbery. Still, he had to do his duty.

There was no sense waiting. 'Mother, I overheard a conversation today between a man and woman. They plan to rob you.'

'Nonsense, Andrew.' She dismissed his warning with a wave of her elegant hand. 'You always were an imaginative child. I had thought you beyond that.'

His jaw clenched before he forcibly relaxed it. This was nothing he had not expected. 'I am, Mother.'

'Well, I cannot believe that anyone in my employ would be so ungrateful as to do what you suggest.'

'Is there someone new who might be in need of money?'

She scowled at him. 'There is Mary Margaret, but her brother-in-law is the curate. She grew up here. Her father was one of my tenants. No, it is not her.'

'Someone else?' he asked, even though his suspicions now lay with the mysterious Mary Margaret. He did not know his mother's tenants, having spent very little time here.

'No, Andrew, there is not.' Exasperation tinged every word. 'But if you insist on this, I shall line up all the servants and demand the guilty party to step forward.'

This was no more than he had expected. He should have known better than to tell his mother. Still, an irritation he rarely allowed himself to feel toward his parent made his next words harsh.

'That would be the worst thing you could do. The thief would be on his guard after that and we would never catch him.'

'Then be done with this nonsense. No one in my employ would do so despicable a thing.' She waved a languid hand, the wrist drooping like a wilted flower. 'I did not summon you here to be told such foolishness.'

Ravensford knew when a subject was ended. To continue pushing her would only make her do up as she threatened. He had not expected her to give credence to his words; she rarely did. He would have to bide his time and catch the pair in the actual act of stealing. Then he would not need his mother's belief or cooperation.

'Now, Andrew,' she continued, her voice light

and musical, 'I asked you to visit for a very specific reason.'

He put the other matter aside for the moment and made himself smile indulgently at her. 'I surmised as much, Mother, and I am at your service. What exactly is it that you wish me to do?'

'My goddaughter, Annabell Winston, needs to have a Season.' She reached for the teapot. 'Do you still take your tea plain?'

'Yes, please.'

In spite of the foreboding edging up his spine, he waited patiently while she poured him a steaming cup of tea. There was no sense prodding her. That route only caused discord without accomplishing any increase in speed or comprehension.

'Now, we shall be arriving in London in early May to give the child plenty of time to assemble an appropriate wardrobe. I expect you to make sure everything is in order.'

He took a swallow of scalding tea and realised that somewhere along his parent's thought processes he had missed something important. 'What exactly do you expect me to do?'

'Really, Andrew, don't be so dense. It isn't like you.' She sipped daintily at her cream-and-sugar-laden drink. 'You are to have the town house properly opened and prepared for us. The ballroom floor very likely needs to be refinished if we are to have a successful coming-out ball for Annabell.'

It was an effort not to groan. The idea of protesting passed through his mind, only to be discarded. His mother had that light in her blue eyes that preceded intense activity—by him.

'And what else am I to do?' he asked, knowing he would not like any part of the answer. His comfortable bachelor life was about to be turned topsy-turvy.

'Oh, very good, Andrew. I knew you would get into the spirit of things once I explained them.' She beamed at him, the charm of her smile identical to his own. 'Vouchers for Almack's are a must. As are invitations to all the private events. The child will likely want to attend Astley's Amphitheatre and all those disgustingly plebian entertainments. Of course, we mustn't forget Covent Garden and Vauxhall.'

Ravensford finished a pastry in one gulp, dreading the answer to his next question. 'And who will be escorting Annabell about since you are not capable of getting out much?'

Her smile widened. 'Why, you, of course. I know how much you enjoy her company and she adores you. Why, the two of you make a perfect couple. It would be delightful if this visit brought about a closer union between you. Your father often said so.'

A twinge of sadness tightened his chest at the mention of his sire, but no matter what his parents had wished, he was not going to marry a miss barely out of the schoolroom. Others might do so, but not he. He preferred women with experience.

'I am not in the market for a wife,' he stated baldly, knowing that nothing short of bluntness got through to his parent and too often not even that.

'So you say.' She leaned gracefully back into the pale yellow silk cushions of her seat, only to bounce forward again. 'I nearly forgot. My companion will help chaperon since it would not be proper for you to escort Annabell alone.'

'Your companion? I thought Miss Mabel left to care for her father.'

'She did, she did. I already told you that I have hired a new companion, Mary Margaret O'Brien.'

Ravensford resisted the urge to shake his head. His mother had mentioned hiring the chit, but not making her a companion. It was the perfect position for a thief. He put the suspicion aside as his mother continued blithely on.

'Quite proper and all, but not of the Quality. Still, a very obliging young woman. She shan't bother you. She is quiet as a mouse.' A complacent smile curved the Countess's lips as she once more leaned back into the plump cushions. 'And her looks are too unusual to be considered attractive. She won't cause you any problems.'

Ravensford narrowed his eyes. In his experience, whenever his mother considered something to be unimportant it ended up being a nightmare. He vividly remembered the litter of puppies she had foisted on him just six months ago. They were supposed to be a *bagatelle*, nothing more. They had ruined his stable and very nearly cost him his head groom. After much cajoling, he had managed to place every pup but one with a good owner. Wizzard ruled Ravensford's country estate with a benign paw. But that was neither here nor there. Right now he had to keep his mother from creating another disaster.

'You do plan on accompanying Annabell whenever possible, don't you?' he asked drily.

'Don't be a goose, Andrew. Of course I do. What kind of godmother would I be otherwise?'

There was no polite answer, so Ravensford made none. Thankfully a tap on the door saved him from his mother's habit of pursuing an answer to her questions.

'Come in,' the Countess said.

Ravensford heard the door open seconds before the faint scent of lavender wafted through the room. Could this be the woman from the library?

His pulse quickened. Still, he did not turn his head to look. Better that he appear completely uninterested.

'My lady,' the newcomer said.

It was she. Her voice purred like that of a contented cat. His gut tightened pleasurably.

Ravensford caught movement from the corner of his eye. Seconds later she was in his line of sight. His entire body responded.

She wore a plain olive-coloured wool gown that hugged the ample curves of her bosom before slipping gracefully past a tiny waist and narrow hips. In profile, her nose was slightly turned up at the tip and her lips were plump and very pink. The watery sun coming through the many-paned window shot blue highlights through her ebony hair which was long, parted in the middle and caught in a severe chignon at the nape of an elegant white neck.

'Mary Margaret,' the Dowager said, 'I asked you here to meet my son, Lord Ravensford. You and he will be spending a great deal of time together in London while you chaperon my goddaughter. My son shall provide the cachet for you to be accepted into the homes of the *ton*.'

Ravensford kept himself from wincing. His mother was not known for her tact. That discomfort faded as the young woman turned to face him.

His mother was right. The chit was not a traditional beauty. She was an exotic temptress.

Her hair lay like a smooth satin cap against her head. He would have likened her to a Madonna because of the demure style and calm scrutiny in her eyes, but there was too much of the unusual in her looks. Her face was heart shaped with winged brows and high cheekbones. Her chin was pointed and with a dainty cleft. But it was her eyes that held him captive. They were green as the finest emeralds and tilted at the corners like a cat's. Her features intensified his impression of her voice, as did her movements when she took a step closer. She was lithe and graceful, flowing like a feline that glides along the ground intent on its own world.

She was amazing. Too bad she was also untrustworthy.

'My lord,' Mary Margaret murmured, making a shallow curtsy.

He rose. 'Please be seated, Miss O'Brien.'

'Thank you.' She took the chair closest to her and sat ramrod straight, yet gracefully as a cat positioning itself to watch the world.

He eased back down and waited to see what more his mother intended and how the woman would react. Much could be told about a person by watching them. It was a trait he had cultivated and which made him very successful in getting some of his less than popular bills through the House of Lords.

'Mary Margaret, we will be staying with my son in London. You will be in charge of completing anything my son has not finished so that the house is ready for us to entertain.'

The woman nodded her head, keeping her huge eyes turned to the Countess. Ravensford found himself wanting to provoke her to speak. He wanted to hear her voice now that he could watch her body and face at the same time. She fascinated him.

'Will you be sending Miss O'Brien ahead, Mother? That would be best if you intend her to make sure that everything is in order.'

It was a provocative idea, and his mother's answer would tell him much about where the Countess placed the woman socially. That she did not think the chit a person of Quality did not mean she thought the girl should alone with a man. Propriety was propriety.

'Why, that is an excellent suggestion,' his mother said. 'I should have thought of it sooner.' She turned her attention to the other woman. 'I believe you should go ahead. Andrew, arrange for Mary Margaret to depart immediately. With luck and good weather, she should be in London within two weeks. That will give her plenty of time.'

Ravensford thought that some colour mounted Miss O'Brien's high cheeks, but she was so composed he could not be sure. She might be his mother's new companion, but his parent did not consider her of consequence. Inexplicably, Ravensford found himself irritated with his mother. She was often oblivious to the feelings of others, and he had thought himself inured to it. It seemed he was not.

'It would be better if I escorted Miss O'Brien. A woman travelling alone is fair game for anyone.'

No respectable woman travelled with a man unchaperoned, but Mary Margaret O'Brien was considered a servant and therefore had no reputation to lose. Even though part of him rose in anger at this lack of regard for the woman, another part of him looked coldly on. She intended to steal from his mother. The trip would allow him to watch her.

The fact that his gut tightened in anticipation was nothing. He must put aside the very physical reminder that she was an enticing woman and remember only that she was a woman out to steal from his mother. That was where his focus should be.

Mary Margaret O'Brien glanced at him, her expression unreadable. She would be a good card player.

Or a good thief.

His mother frowned. 'I really don't see that your presence is necessary. Several outriders will do just as well.'

Ravensford looked blandly at his mother. 'I disagree. It's obvious that Miss O'Brien is gently reared or you would not have her for a companion. The trip to London is long and not always safe. I must insist on accompanying her.'

His mother's frown turned to a glare. It was not often that he refused to do her bidding.

'If you insist,' she said ungraciously. She stood up and moved to the fireplace where the bell pull was, casting Ravensford a you-will-pay look. 'The two of you should not linger here. There is much too much to be done. I will order the travelling carriage to be readied for departure tomorrow morning.'

Ravensford groaned. He should have known that, once he insisted on thwarting her, she would make the result as unpleasant as possible. That was her way of seeing that he did not refuse her in the future. She had used that method on him all his life and it usually worked.

He remembered the time shortly after his father died when he had suggested they have Raven Abbey modernised. She had not wanted anything changed. To her Raven Abbey was a symbol of her life with her husband. But Ravensford had insisted. Before he had even had time enough to determine whom the architect should be and what should be done, the Countess had hired Nash and determined the entire structure should be redone in the Egyptian mode so popular at the time. He still had difficulty visiting his country seat.

During the entire exchange, Miss O'Brien had looked straight ahead. Never once had she so much as glanced at the two people who were deciding her immediate future. He would have felt like chattel. Part of him rebelled at what they were doing to her.

'You are dismissed, Mary Margaret,' the Countess said haughtily. 'I am sure you have much to do before you leave.'

Miss O'Brien rose quickly and curtsied to the Countess. 'My lady. I shall be ready whenever you wish.' Then as though reluctant, she turned to him and dipped down. 'My lord.'

He rose quickly. 'I will send a maid to help you pack.'

Her incredible eyes widened momentarily. 'That won't be necessary, my lord. I have little to take and nothing I cannot pack myself.'

He met her calm gaze. 'Someone will help you.'

'Really, Andrew, don't be importunate,' his mother said, only barely covering her disapproval with disdain.

Ravensford ignored his parent.

Miss O'Brien bowed her head in acceptance even though Ravensford sensed that the chit was far from compliant. 'Thank you, my lord.'

'You may go, Mary Margaret,' the Countess said coldly.

A flash of what might have been anger entered the younger woman's eyes, but was gone so quickly that Ravensford decided he had been mistaken. He would not have blamed her had she taken offense at his mother's words and tone.

He watched her leave the room, intrigued by her walk. Tall and regal, she held herself as though a book balanced on the top of her head. She was magnificent. Too bad she was employed by his parent. Otherwise he would offer a *carte blanche* and the devil take the results.

No woman had ever made him react this strongly. Try as he might, the idea of her in his arms and in his bed created an unquenchable fire in his loins.

'Andrew!'

He turned his attention back to his mother. 'Yes?' he asked, pretending that he saw nothing unusual in her command.

'The girl is nobody. She does not need your attentions or your help. Leave her alone.'

Irritation tightened the corners of his mouth. His mother was used to having her way. 'I do not intend to do her harm.'

'See that it remains that way.' The Countess chopped her normally languid hand. 'Now be gone. I must rest.'

Ravensford made an ironic bow and left. He would arrange for a maid to help Miss O'Brien, a loyal servant who had been in his mother's employ for years, despite what his mother and the girl wanted. Perhaps his mother's personal maid, Jane. She would know if anything in Miss O'Brien's possessions really belonged to his mother, and she would come to him immediately if that were the case.

Chapter Two

Mary Margaret left the drawing room as sedately as her thumping heart would let her. Behind her the Countess and Earl talked as though they were alone. To them, she was a servant, and the aristocracy talked in front of their servants as though they did not exist.

She carefully closed the heavy door. The butler stood nearby, waiting for orders. She smiled at him before turning and hurrying down the hall toward the servants' stairs and the back entrance.

She had to tell Thomas immediately. He would be furious. Nor did she want to go to London. This was home and she had never been farther than the nearby village of Cashel.

And there were Emily and Annie to take care of.

She rushed out the door, not bothering with a

cape, and sped down the path that led to the trail through the pastures. As curate, Thomas had a small cottage near the church. She hoped he would be there and if not, then at the church.

She was out of breath when she got there. She pounded impatiently on the door. After what seemed an eternity, Annie answered.

Her niece was small for her age, with large green eyes, a pointed chin and a wealth of black hair. She had been crying.

Mary Margaret fell to her knees and gathered the child in her arms. She stroked back the long hair, dread filling her. 'What is the matter, sweetheart?'

'Hiccup.' Annie squirmed away and rubbed at her eyes. 'Daddy...was angry.'

Mary Margaret closed her own eyes, wishing she could blot out the misery in her niece's and knowing she could not. 'Where is your mama?'

Annie jerked her head toward the bedroom.

'Stay here, sweetheart,' Mary Margaret said calmly, even though she was far from calm. The last thing she wanted was to upset Annie further.

As curate, Thomas had a modest cottage. The large rectory was occupied by the parish minister. Thomas had spent many afternoons and Sundays trying to ingratiate himself into the Countess's good graces in the hope that she would provide him with his own living. So far, he was unsuccessful. That was just one of the reasons Thomas wanted her to steal for him.

She knocked before entering the room. Her only sister sat hunched on the bed, one hand cradling her cheek. Mary Margaret rushed to her.

'Oh, Emily. Let me see.' She pulled Emily's hand away and frowned. 'You will have a bruise.'

'I walked into the door.'

Mary Margaret moved away to the water basin where she wet a cloth. Taking it back to her sister, she said, 'No, you did not. Thomas hit you. But why?'

Emily refused to meet Mary Margaret's eyes. Compassion and anger warred in Mary Margaret. Emily had been a beauty, her hair dark as a raven's wing and her eyes blue as the sky. Now she was worn beyond her twenty-six years. Mary Margaret hated Thomas Fox, hated him with a passion that, in her calmer moments, shamed her.

Emily shrugged. 'Who knows?'

Mary Margaret was afraid she did. He had not liked her defiance. What would he do now?

'Emily, leave him. Come away with me. We will take Annie.'

'And go where? Neither of us has money to even feed ourselves for one day, let alone care for a child.' Bitterness tinged every word. 'No, I must stay. At least Annie is fed and clothed and has a roof over her head.'

'Come to the big house with me.'

'Ha! The Countess cares less than nothing for the likes of us.'

'But the Earl is here. They say he is compassionate, and so he seemed.'

A slight gleam of interest entered Emily's dull eyes. 'The Earl is here? Perhaps that is why Thomas was angry. He might fear that the Earl will take his mother away and just when Thomas is getting close enough to ask her for a better living.'

She had not thought of that and her fear mounted. He would be furious when he found out that they were all leaving for London shortly. Unconsciously she started wringing her hands.

'Oh, dear, Emily.' She fell to her knees in front of her sister and grasped Emily's hands. 'Please, please come away with me now. Please.'

'Why?'

'We are all leaving. The Earl, the Countess, and…me. Going to London.' She rushed on. 'I have a little put aside. I will send you more when I get my first quarterly salary.'

Emily sagged. 'I have nowhere to go.'

Desperate as she was, Mary Margaret knew Emily was right. There was nowhere to go. No one would believe that the saintly, wonderful Mr Fox beat his wife. Not even the vicar. Nor could she go to the Countess. As Emily had said, the woman would not care.

Wearily she stood. 'Where is Thomas? I must tell him.'

Emily sighed. 'At the church.'

Feeling more defeated than when her parents had both suddenly died of influenza and she had had to shoulder the burden of caring for her younger sister, Mary Margaret trudged from the room. The church was only a five-minute walk away.

She entered the darkened sanctuary and had to give her eyes several moments to adjust. Thomas was at the front talking to Mrs Smith, one of the farmers' wives. Mary Margaret sat on the nearest wooden bench to wait.

When Thomas finally headed her way, she could tell by his walk that he was furious. She gulped back her fear and resisted the urge to flee. Unpleasant as her news was, she had to tell him.

He stopped short of her, arms akimbo. He looked like a golden god towering above her. With his blue eyes, sun-bright hair, perfect physique and immaculate grooming, he looked to be everything a woman could want and everything a parish could desire in their spiritual leader. How false.

Unbidden, the image of the Earl formed. He was

not breathtakingly handsome as Thomas was. Ravensford was rugged, more earthlike in his masculine appeal, with auburn hair and piercing green eyes. He was also more powerfully built, giving a sense of protection to those around him—or so she had felt. He was oddly disturbing to her.

'Why are you here?'

Thomas's demand effectively ended Mary Margaret's thoughts. She stood, not willing to have him lord it over her.

Taking a deep breath, she rushed the words. 'The Countess, the Earl and I are leaving for London immediately.'

'What?' His voice filled the tiny church, echoing off the centuries-old stone walls.

It was all Mary Margaret could do not to cringe. She had learned to fear Thomas's anger.

'The Countess is taking her goddaughter to London for a Season. I am to go ahead with the Earl to prepare the town house.'

Thomas's hand moved as though he meant to slap her. Mary Margaret stepped back. How could they have ever thought him the answer to Emily's prayers? How his charm and seeming devotion to her sister had fooled them.

'When?'

'Tomorrow. The Countess is to follow.'

He paced away, his boots ringing on the stone

floor. Coming back, he ordered, 'Do as the Countess wishes. There are bound to be more opportunities in London for you to steal from her.'

Mary Margaret blanched. She had secretly hoped he would tell her to quit, that London was too far away and did him no good.

When she spoke she was glad her voice did not quaver. 'But how shall I get home? Even if I do manage to get her jewels, I don't know how to get back from London.'

His fine mouth sneered. 'That is your problem, one you will solve since Emily and Annie will be here.'

His implied threat was only what she had expected. He knew she would manage somehow to keep him from hurting them more. He was ordering her to do an immoral and illegal act. Even though she hoped to thwart him and still save her sister and niece, the anger toward him that she usually held in check burst out.

'If you harm them, if you so much as lay a finger on Annie or hit Emily again, I shall turn myself into the authorities and I shall tell them all about you.'

He laughed. 'Very noble. But no one will believe your story about me. I am the younger son of Viscount Fox. It would be your word against mine—and you are nobody.'

The sense of defeat gnawed at her. She fought it off. 'They might not believe me, but it would do your reputation no good to have the accusation made public.'

His narrowed eyes told her she had finally succeeded in getting past his armour. 'Do so and I will make you rue the instant you opened your mouth.'

She never doubted him. Her hands clenched in the folds of her gown.

'Now, get out of here. I will be waiting for your first report and your final return.'

His cold words washed over her nerves like a scratch on a blackboard. She was defeated. Again.

She retraced her steps to Derry House. She came even with the Gothic folly the Countess had built last summer. Honeysuckle mingled with climbing roses, acting like curtains for the structure's windows. Soon they would bloom and their scents would fill the air. A brook raced along behind. Birds cavorted overhead and roosted in the eaves. It was a haven she had frequently gone to during her short time with the Countess.

Her feet took her toward it now.

She reached the door just as a rustle caught her attention, followed by a shadow disengaging from an interior wall. Her heart thumped and her left hand rose to her throat.

'Miss O'Brien,' a male baritone said.

She recognised the Earl's voice instantly. The deep tone slid like velvet along her senses. Even in the dim, filtered light she could see the glint of his copper hair. His teeth were a bared white slash.

She forced herself to relax. Her hand fell to her side and her breathing evened out. 'My lord.'

He advanced on her until he was close enough that she imagined she could feel the heat from his body. Awareness of him rose within her like a tidal wave reaching for the full moon. She shivered.

'Do you come here often?' His tone was conversational, yet she thought she detected an underlying current of interest. But why?

'When I feel the need for privacy.' She answered him bluntly and boldly, knowing she should be more respectful, yet needing that privacy very much. He was too disturbing, increasing her discomfort.

Instead of finding solace in her hidey-hole, she was finding a very disquieting part of her nature. Since watching her sister fall in love with a man like Thomas Fox, Mary Margaret had made herself impervious to men. The Earl was slipping past her barrier. Even his voice aroused her senses. What would it be like if he touched her?

Shocked at her own forwardness in even thinking such a thing, she drew herself straight. Proper ladies did not have such thoughts, not even ladies born of yeoman farmers.

'And you wish me at the devil instead of invading your solitude,' he murmured, a hint of amusement making his voice rich and creamy.

'I had hoped to be alone,' she said, keeping her tone even in spite of the tremors shifting through her body.

She was never this bold, but desperation drove her. He disturbed her too much, and she needed time to think through what she was going to do. Relief flooded her when he moved forward, as though to pass her and go out the door that was behind her. The relief was short lived.

He stopped beside her, close enough that she could feel his warm breath. She had never been this close to a man who was not family. She licked suddenly dry lips.

'You look upset, Miss O'Brien. Is there anything I can do?'

Her eyes widened. He sounded genuinely concerned. For a moment, but not longer, she found herself tempted to pour out her problem. He was a powerful man. He could help her, help her sister and niece, if he chose. Then the moment was gone.

She had heard many things about this man standing too close to her. The young female servants said he was known for his mistresses and his charm. The men admired his abilities in sports. He was what the fashionable called a Corinthian. She had even heard that he was a champion of the downtrodden.

All she could think of was that he was the Countess's son, and the Countess cared nothing for those beneath her.

No, no matter how tempting the Earl made his question sound, she would not answer. She had too much to lose and, as far as she knew, nothing to gain by confiding in him.

'Thank you for your concern, my lord, but I am fine. I am a solitary person, that is all.'

His eyes met and held hers for a long time. She realised with a thrill of apprehension that she could not make herself look away. For her, he was more dangerous than Thomas.

'Then I shall leave you.' He nodded before sauntering from the building.

Mary Margaret barely made it to one of several chairs positioned around the folly before her legs gave out. She gripped the arms until her knuckles turned white and she lost feeling in her fingers. If she reacted this strongly to him after such a brief exposure, how was she going to survive the trip to London in his company? This was madness.

And yet…was this how Emily had felt the first time she saw Thomas? She had never understood

Emily's immediate attraction to Thomas, and when they had wed after only knowing each other a month she had been shocked. Perhaps now she could understand.

But none of this solved her problem. Even with the threat to Emily and Annie, she was not sure she could bring herself to steal from the Countess. In the back of her mind, she had hoped to devise a plan that would outsmart Thomas. So far, she had not.

She chewed her bottom lip.

This trip to London might be better than she had thought. It would give her time to formulate something without having Thomas constantly coming upon her and demanding that she act immediately or he would hurt her sister. Not even Thomas could be so impatient as not to realise how much more time it would take to gain access to the Countess's jewels now that she was going to London. It was her only hope.

She rose with a sigh. Tired as she was, she still had to pack her meagre belongings. The day was nearly over and tomorrow would be here all too soon.

She made her way to the manor's back entrance. From there, she climbed the servants' stairs to the third floor. Wearily, she pushed open the door to her room and froze.

'What are you doing here?'

Jane, the Countess's personal maid, looked over her plump shoulder. She was a round woman, her apple-red face as full as the rest. Iron-grey hair worn pulled tightly back made her look like a dumpling. She was not the merry character her person resembled.

'What are you gaping at, girl?' Jane demanded.

Mary Margaret tamped down on the anger brought about by this invasion of privacy. 'Who let you in?'

'Don't be daft. I let myself in.' Jane straightened out and turned to face Mary Margaret.

'I told the Earl that I don't require help to pack.'

Jane snorted, her full mouth and button nose prominent. 'His lordship does as he pleases. He ordered me here even though waiting on you is beneath me.' She cast an unfriendly look at Mary Margaret. 'Don't be thinking you're better than you are. The Earl is in a hurry to do his mother's bidding, missy.'

She turned her back on Mary Margaret and marched to the plain oak dresser. She pulled out the few neatly folded clothes and eyed them with a jaundiced look. 'Least they are clean.'

Mary Margaret had done her best to tolerate this invasion, but this last was too much. 'They are more than clean. They are decent and come by

honestly. More than some can say.' She stalked to
the other woman and took the maligned clothing
from Jane's plump fingers. 'I do not need your
disparaging comments or your help. Please leave.'

Jane's brown eyes narrowed and her lips
thinned. 'Don't be getting above yourself, missy.'

Seeing that she was only making matters worse,
Mary Margaret tried another track. 'I know my
place very well, and I am far beneath your notice.
You are a busy woman and have other things to
do. My meagre packing should not detain you.'

'True,' Jane said with a haughty sniff. 'But if I
don't help, his lordship won't be happy.'

Mary Margaret considered the Earl for a minute.
He was the source of quite a bit of her uneasiness,
and she liked him less by the instant. 'He will live.
Surely I am not the first person during his lifetime
to refuse his bidding.'

'That's as may be. *I* have never gone against his
lordship's orders unless my lady has bid me differently.'

'I have no doubt of it,' Mary Margaret murmured, weary of the confrontation and the conversation. They went in circles. 'Perhaps it would be
enough for you to see my few belongings.'

Jane looked down her tiny nose as Mary Margaret took out the remainder of her belongings and
spread them on the narrow bed. A travelling dress,

two day dresses, boots, pattens, one pair of slippers, a nightdress with a plain robe, and underclothes completed her wardrobe.

'What about jewellery?'

Mary Margaret pulled a simple gold locket from beneath the collar of her dress. Inside were tiny pictures of her parents. 'Only this.'

Jane looked disdainfully at the unadorned piece. 'Anything else?'

Mary Margaret curled her fingers protectively around the locket. It was all she had left of her parents. The farm her father had worked had passed to someone upon his death, the furniture and personal items going to pay debts and hers and Emily's education with the vicar where Emily had met Thomas. She pushed away the painful memories of loss and regret.

'No, I have nothing else,' Mary Margaret said. 'Except my portmanteau. Would you care to examine it? Or watch while I pack?'

Jane took the only chair, her ample dimensions flowing over the sides. 'I will watch.'

Mary Margaret bit back a sharp retort and started folding clothes. The sooner she was done the sooner she would be alone. Minutes later, she stuffed the last item into the now full portmanteau.

'Harumph! You will never get the wrinkles out,' Jane stated, standing.

'I will manage. I am, after all, merely a servant, and not even an important one.'

'True.'

Without another word, Jane left, her ample form squeezing through the sides of the door. Mary Margaret released a sigh.

Why did the Earl care about her packing? It seemed such a small and silly thing for him to be concerned about.

He was very disconcerting, as was her reaction to him. If he told her to do something, she would be hard pressed to refuse him simply because she found him so mesmerising. Hopefully she would see very little of him. Most gentlemen did not like travelling in a carriage, so he would probably ride most of the trip. In London he would be too busy to pay attention to her.

She rose and went to the single window. Using her handkerchief, she rubbed a spot clean and gazed out at the immaculately groomed garden. Green speckled with other colours met her eye. Above, clouds scudded across a pale blue sky. This evening would bring rain. Nothing unusual in Ireland. Spring was her favourite time of the year, a time of new beginnings and birth.

How she wished Emily would run away with her and start anew. But so far she refused. And because of that, Mary Margaret had to do as Thomas ordered. When she had initially refused his orders, he had threatened to do more than blacken Emily's eye or Annie's jaw. So she had agreed. But somehow she would thwart him and get Emily and Annie from him. No matter that the law said a wife was her husband's property and a daughter the same until given to another man in marriage.

A robin flew by the window, its little chest covered by a red vest, and alighted on the nearby tree. His colourful feathers reminded her once more of the Earl of Ravensford.

He was a ruggedly handsome man, not at all classical in looks. His eyes sparkled with something deeper than humour that was more compelling than mere charm, although she was sure that he had more than his fair share of that attribute. Then there was his mouth that hinted at passions she could only guess about. When he had spoken to her, she had been hard pressed not to lose herself in the fantasy of his lips on hers. A silly thought and totally impossible.

She sighed at her own weakness, her finger tracing a pattern in the glass. Before she quite realised what she had done, there was a man's profile etched in the window.

With the strong, patrician nose, the picture could only be of Ravensford. He was a forceful man, used to having his own way. She also knew he could be dangerous for her.

She put her palm to the glass and smeared out the image. If only she could as easily banish him from her mind. Everything seemed to lead back to him.

With a sigh, she turned away. These melancholy thoughts helped no one, and tomorrow she began her long journey to London with the Earl as her protector.

A shiver chased down her spine. From fear or anticipation, she knew not, only that she felt alive as never before.

Chapter Three

Stone-grey clouds scuttled across the early morning sky. Damp, cold wind rippled through the trees and whipped Mary Margaret's cape into a frenzy about her legs.

She started down the first marble step, wondering when the Countess would appear and order her to return inside the house and go out the servants' entrance. The Countess had done that Mary Margaret's first day. The butler and footmen had watched impassively, but one of the young female servants had snickered. Mary Margaret had not made that mistake again—until today. It was nerves.

The travelling carriage, with whatever the Earl and his mother had thought necessary, waited on the gravel outside the front entry, scant yards from her. The horses champed at the bit and pawed the ground, their breath mist on the rising wind. It would storm soon, spring forgotten in winter's dying hand. Travel would be hard.

In her hurry, she tripped in her skirts. Her feet skidded on the slick stone, and she pitched forward. The hard marble raced toward her face. She flung a hand up to break her fall, dropping her portmanteau.

An arm like a band of iron wrapped around her waist. A firm hand caught her elbow and helped steady her. In seconds she was pressed against an unyielding chest.

She took a breath to still her beating heart, knowing she had been saved from a nasty accident. Thinking herself once more in charge of her emotions, she tried to move away from the man who held her. The grip tightened so that she twisted in the no longer needed embrace, intending to set the importunate person in his place. She might not be a lady of Quality, but she was a lady and no lady was held so intimately by a man who was not her father, brother or husband.

Eyes the colour of newly scythed grass met hers. A mouth she had thought sensual yesterday curved into a wicked smile, showing a dimple in the left cheek that threatened to weaken her knees. Still, the Earl's grip on her waist did not loosen. If anything, it tightened.

The look he bent on her took another turn, becoming slumberous and intense. Awareness of his body pressed so tightly to hers shivered along her every nerve.

After an eternity, his arm slid away, gliding along the curve of her waist and skirting the swell of her hips. It was nearly a caress and she felt it through all the layers of her dress, pelisse and cape. Heat threatened to engulf her entire being.

She forced her eyes to look away from his and her knees to bend in a curtsy. 'Thank you, my lord,' she murmured, not sure what she thanked him for. Part of her mind knew he had saved her from a disastrous fall, yet another part of her mind understood that he had awakened something in her that had been dormant. 'Thank you for stopping my fall,' she said at last.

'You are welcome,' he said, his voice low and husky as though he had an inflammation of the lungs. He had not sounded this way yesterday.

'Are you unwell, my lord?' she blurted.

His smile became rueful. 'Nothing so mundane. Let me help you down the rest of these steps. They are treacherous in weather such as this, and it would not suit my mother to have you injured and forced to remain here.'

He spoke the truth, yet she sensed more beneath his words. Instantly she scolded herself. His hand still held her elbow and it made reasonable thinking hard. Her reaction to him scared her. Scared her as nothing else ever had.

'Thank you, my lord,' she murmured once again. 'But I am on my guard now and able to care for myself.'

She bent to retrieve her portmanteau. His hand was before hers.

'I can carry it.'

'I am sure you can, but I shall do so.'

He gave her a mocking half-bow that brought the blush of embarrassment to her cheeks. What would the other servants say about this? What would his mother say when she heard the gossip? The Countess would not be pleased. Perhaps it was just as well that she was leaving.

From beneath her lashes, she watched Ravensford hand her portmanteau to a footman. His shoulders appeared broader than yesterday, the many capes of his coat accentuating them. His hair sparkled like copper even in the dull light coming through the clouds. She shook herself in an effort to dispel his draw.

He turned at that moment. 'You are cold. Get inside the coach. There are blankets and heated stones. A bottle full of hot water as well. Another full of hot chocolate.'

'Are you travelling in the carriage, my lord?' All those comforts could not be for her.

'Later. Perhaps.'

He helped her into the carriage, his hand lingering. Her gaze went to his touch before rising to his face. The look he gave her was one she did not understand, but knew instinctively meant danger to her.

He released her. 'Drink all the hot chocolate. It will help keep you warm until we stop for lunch.'

She looked at him. 'Surely it is for you.'

'I think not.' He chuckled. 'Too sweet for my tastes. I like a drink that burns its way down and keeps me warm.'

Almost she thought he meant something besides what his words said. In her fancy, she could think he spoke a special language just for her. This would not do.

She fell back on the security of protocol. 'Thank you, my lord.'

He gave her a quizzical look before turning away. She breathed a sigh of relief. His regard was too disturbing.

Ravensford made his way to his mount. Could a woman with a voice and looks such as hers truly be the innocent she portrayed? Or was this all part of her plan to steal from his mother? Both were questions he could not answer yet, but he would eventually, no matter what he had to do.

Ravensford mounted, and with a wave of his hand to the groom holding the horse's reins, he set out. It would be a long journey.

He glanced back once, wondering if his mother was up and watching. No pale face looked out from a window. The Countess was still abed, as he had expected.

The weather rapidly worsened, and Ravensford considered riding in the carriage—a big lumbering vehicle designed to carry luggage, not people who were in a hurry. And they were in a hurry. There was much to be done to his town house in order to bring it up to his mother's standards and very little time to do it in.

Riding his horse and getting drenched to the bone would accomplish nothing, while if he rode inside he would be able to question Miss O'Brien about herself and her future. Not to mention take in his fill of her exotic features. The last was a consideration he pushed from his mind. His duty was to learn enough to outfox her, not to become entangled with her.

He signalled the coachman and outriders to stop. His mount was tied to the back of the vehicle and the ancient steps let down. Ravensford entered in time to see the woman hurriedly stuff something under the neck of her gown, as though she did not wish him to see whatever it was. He wondered if it was something to do with her mission.

Mary Margaret saw the Earl's gaze on her neck. Homesick already, she had been gazing at the pictures of her parents in her locket. The moment was too personal to share with someone she did not know, so when she had heard the coach door open, she had put the locket back.

Warily, she watched the Earl take the seat opposite her, back to the horses, and make himself comfortable. She had not thought he would join her, no matter how awful the weather became.

'I thought gentlemen preferred to ride,' she said. 'Nor should you be the one to sit facing away from the horses.'

His right eyebrow rose, a burnt slash across his broad brow. 'Gentlemen do as they please, and it pleases me to get inside away from the wind and rain and to sit where I am. 'Tis too bad the others cannot do the same. I would call a halt if I thought this storm would let up soon. Unfortunately, it looks to follow us to the coast.'

Mary Margaret felt her mouth drop in surprise. 'You care about their discomfort?'

Ravensford frowned. 'They are human beings, are they not?'

She nodded, clamping her teeth shut. She had

already more than overstepped the gap between an earl and a tenant farmer's daughter. She did not need to compound her error with more inane comments.

Silence fell, but she was intensely, painfully aware of his nearness. She could hear him breathing and cast him fleeting glances from beneath her lashes. He lounged at his leisure, or as much as was possible with the carriage swaying from side to side and jolting with every numerous hole in the road. His right hand gripped the leather strap for stability. He had long fingers, covered by riding gloves.

She saw his muscles bunch beneath the folds of his coat. Confusion spread through her as she remembered the strength in his circling arm when he had caught her up. No man had ever held her so close, yet it had felt right—and exciting.

She turned her head sharply, hoping to forget the sensation of his touch by looking anywhere but at him. He was a disturbing man. More so because of what she had to do—unless she could outwit her brother-in-law.

'What do you see in the rain that is so interesting?'

His voice was deep with the refined tones of the British aristocracy. Yet there was more to it than that. There was a warmth that seemed to stroke her nerves, heightening her senses.

She shook her head at her fancifulness. This had to stop. He was so far above her as to be as unattainable as the sun. Not that she wanted him. She was not so susceptible nor so stupid as to let her imagination run that wild.

He probably treated his women poorly. He certainly would never marry such as herself, and she would never be a man's mistress—not that he had asked or even intended to do so. So, there it was. She was being overly silly and all because he was handsome and had a voice that made her insides feel like warm pudding.

She said the first safe thing that popped into her head. 'We shall have to stop soon if this rain continues. The road is becoming a morass.'

'True.'

He leaned forward to look out the window, moving so close to her that she felt stifled. She wondered if he did so on purpose, if he knew how his proximity affected her. She drew back, putting as much distance between them as the confines would allow. He shot her a glance that in her mind seemed to say he knew how disturbing his nearness was.

'I am hoping to reach a small inn on the outskirts of the next town. At least there we can stable the horses and all get warm food and a place to sleep.'

Instead of shifting back to his place, he stayed watching out the window. The dim carriage lamp showed his profile, his arrogant nose a-jut and his jaw a firm statement of strength. Golden stubble dotted his face, surprising her. She had thought he would grow a red beard because of his hair. She was wrong.

After her heart had raced itself to a near stop in sheer exhaustion, he finally sat back. He slanted her a speculative glance. She met his study with as much aplomb as she could dredge up. She had never been uncomfortable around men, but she was with him. Her skin prickled and her imagination ran amok, neither one being a condition she enjoyed, or so she told herself.

'I hope you won't find the lack of comforts at this place too much of a hardship, Miss O'Brien.'

That was the last thing she had expected him to be concerned about. 'Me? I should think your lordship will have a greater problem than me.'

A bitter smile twisted his fine mouth. 'I bivouacked in the Peninsula. I am used to Spartan accommodations. It is you I am concerned for.'

Was he baiting her? And if so, why should he think this would do so? 'I am sure you are, my lord. However, I too am used to not being coddled.'

'Really? Where did you live before coming to stay with my mother?'

His voice showed only mild interest, yet Mary Margaret was instantly on her guard. There was no reason a man of his standing should be interested in her past. But once the question was asked, there was no reason to lie. She would tell him her life's story, except for Thomas's treatment of Emily, and the Earl would quickly find himself bored.

'I am the oldest daughter of one of your mother's tenant farmers. My parents are gone and my sister is married.'

He picked up the earthenware container of hot chocolate. 'Would you care for some, Miss O'Brien?'

The abrupt change in conversation nonplussed her. 'Please.'

Somehow he managed to pour her a cup without spilling the liquid. She took it, startled by the shock when her fingers accidentally brushed his. The jolt felt like the spark caused when her feet brushed along a carpet and then she touched something.

'You are very well-spoken for a tenant farmer's daughter,' he said while she took a sip of the hot chocolate.

She wondered if he always jumped from topic to topic. It was very disconcerting.

'My mother's father was a vicar. She…married beneath her. She taught us diction and everything she knew. When her knowledge ran out, she did chores for Reverend Hopkins in exchange for lessons in Greek and Latin for us.'

'Who is us?'

'My sister Emily and myself.'

'You are very well educated. Most women of my acquaintance are only barely conversant in those languages. Many can't even speak French fluently.'

His praise embarrassed her. She was not used to compliments in any form, let alone from someone of his position. His mother certainly had not thought her accomplishments worth much.

By the time her first quarter with the Countess was over, she would have barely enough to keep herself and Emily for a year and that was if they lived as frugally as their upbringing had taught them and did small chores in exchange for food. Still, they would manage. They had to.

Thankfully, the carriage lurched because she had no answer to his praise. The liquid in her cup sloshed over the rim and on to her lap. She bounced forward as the vehicle stopped.

For the second time in one day, she found herself in the Earl's arms. If it were not so disturbing to her peace of mind and calmness of body, she would find it amusing. As it was, she could barely breathe. His face was too close, his arms too tight, and his lips too enticing.

'Catching you seems to be my job today,' he murmured, continuing to hold her.

She stared up at him, a distant part of her awareness wondering why he did not release her. The majority of her awareness thrilled to his touch.

She watched as his gaze travelled from her eyes to her mouth. Hunger, or some other strong emotion she could not name, drew harsh lines in his cheeks. If she didn't know better, she would think he intended to kiss her. She was being silly.

His face lowered until his warm breath caressed her skin. The scent of lemons and musk filled her senses. She knew she should struggle. She was not the type of woman men kissed unless their intentions were less than honourable. She had nothing to offer and no family to defend her.

His mouth skimmed hers and she melted against him, knowing even as she did so that she was making a terrible mistake.

'My lord,' a male voice said from outside the coach.

Ravensford thrust her away so quickly Mary Margaret's head swam. She blinked several times in a vain attempt to clear her senses.

'My lord, we are stuck solid in the mud.'

'Damnation, I was afraid of that,' the Earl said, opening the carriage door and jumping out without a backward glance at Mary Margaret.

Unconsciously, the trembling fingers of one hand went to her mouth. He had nearly kissed her. His lips had brushed hers. She still felt weak as a kitten. He had such power over her without even trying.

Taking a deep breath, she composed herself as best she could. She pulled a handkerchief from her reticule and dabbed half-heartedly at the spill of chocolate that had started the whole episode.

From the open door came the sounds of men cursing. She edged to the door and looked out. The back wheel on her side was sunk up to the axle in mud. The two outriders, the groom and coachman were all trying to lever the wheel out of the hole. She knew her weight was not making their effort any easier.

Gathering her cape close around her neck, Mary Margaret leapt from the carriage to what had once been the dirt road. She landed with a splat and sank several inches. Rain pelted her. Thank goodness the wind had stopped or the weather would be truly beastly. As it was, she was a country girl and could stand in this rain for hours if need be.

'What do you think you are doing?' the Earl demanded, stalking toward her. He stopped barely a foot from her, his face a mask of irritation.

His angry voice surprised her. 'I am getting out of the carriage to lighten the load,' she said in a voice that implied that her action was self-evident. Still, she backed away.

'Get back in.'

'When they are done,' she said calmly, hoping the quiver she felt didn't sound in her voice.

'Get back in or I shall be forced to throw you in.'

She edged back, the mud sucking at her feet and making movement difficult. 'I am used to weather like this. Besides, without my weight the work will go quicker. This is better for everyone. I should feel badly if my staying dry in the carriage meant everyone else had to work harder and longer than necessary.'

'Very noble,' he said sarcastically. 'But I meant what I said. There is no reason for you to suffer like this.'

While he spoke, he stripped off his great coat and then his inner coat until he stood in his shirt. The rain instantly plastered the fine linen to his body.

Try as she would, Mary Margaret could not keep from looking at his chest. Muscles rippled beneath the soaked material, and his shoulders looked broad enough to bear the weight of the coach without help from anyone else.

'Miss O'Brien,' Ravensford said dangerously. He took several steps toward her.

The sound of her name grabbed her attention and she looked up at his face. His eyes seemed to spark in the grey light. Had he seen where her attention had been focussed? She hoped not. She would be too humiliated if he had.

He loomed over her. Dimly she perceived that the other men were watching them, waiting to see what would happen. Her hair had loosened in sodden ropes and she pushed them off her face. The Earl's hair dripped water down his face. They were both being ridiculously stubborn and doing no one any good.

She knew defeat when he stood scowling down at her. She turned and scampered back into the carriage as best she could with mud clinging to her boots like a lover clings to his fleeing mistress. A fanciful thought if she had ever had one, she decided, once she was safely inside the vehicle and away from the Earl's menacing presence.

The rain beat on the roof in rhythm to the men rocking the carriage. Mary Margaret clenched her teeth and hands, hoping they would succeed soon. Everyone was going to be cold, wet and dirty.

A sudden jolt and lurch accompanied by a loud sucking sound told her they were free. She relaxed against the squabs, only belatedly realising her soaked clothing would ruin the velvet cloth. She pealed off her cape and spread it on the seat beside her. The Earl would be joining her soon and they would continue on their way.

The coach moved slowly forward.

Seconds dragged into long minutes and Ravensford did not appear. She looked out the window and saw him mounted on his horse, his coats on once more. His beaver hat provided his face a modicum of protection from the steady downpour.

She relaxed back on to the seat with a sigh, torn between irritation that he was riding in the awful weather and relief that he was not sitting in the carriage with her. She sat engrossed in her confused thoughts until the carriage finally rumbled to a halt.

She quickly realised they must be at the inn that was the Earl's destination. Ravensford himself opened the door and extended his hand to help her out. Reluctantly, she put her fingers into his and met his eyes. His anger sparked at her, and she realised that a confrontation with the Earl lay ahead. And all because she had tried to help.

Chapter Four

The rain pelted her face as she looked defiantly up at Ravensford. His hair dripped water beneath the brim of his beaver hat. Lines radiated from his eyes. On most men of his station the creases would be the results of too many long nights spent gaming, wenching and drinking. She doubted he was any different. The knowledge was small comfort.

When she hesitated, he nearly yanked her from the coach. She gasped and put her free arm on his chest to keep herself from tumbling.

'When I tell you to do something, Miss O'Brien, I mean exactly that.'

'Yes, my lord,' she muttered, twisting her arm in a vain attempt to free it.

'Here,' he said, releasing her while using his one hand to unclasp his great coat. He shrugged out of it and swung it around her.

'I cannot.'

She reached to pluck it from her shoulders, but his hands gripped hers. His eyes blazed down at her.

'What did I just say?'

'I have forgotten,' she said in a spurt of unusual rebellion.

'No, you have not.'

He fastened the top button before grabbing her again and urging her toward the inn's door. The dried dirt on her hem and shoes quickly became mud again. She noticed that his Hessians were coated.

The door opened before the Earl could grasp the handle and a round, squat man stood before them and tisked.

'My lord, I was not expecting you,' the proprietor said, his hands wiping futilely at his pristine white apron.

'I am sorry to discommode you, Littleton. I had hoped to make the coast this evening and therefore not need your services. This storm put paid to that.'

The innkeeper nodded before turning and leading them down a narrow hall. 'My parlour is unoccupied, my lord.'

At the Earl's prodding, Mary Margaret followed the owner to a small room where a fire blazed.

Heat engulfed her. Warm, welcome heat that made her garments steam and smell of wet wool.

'Please, my lord, I will send a girl to fetch your coat for cleaning. And soon—'

'Whiskey for me and tea for the lady,' Ravensford said, interrupting. 'And whatever you are cooking. See that my servants are cared for as well.'

'Yes, my lord. Mutton and potatoes. Ale as well for the others.'

'Plenty of it, Littleton.'

'Yes, my lord.'

The landlord was barely out of the door when Ravensford turned on her. 'Take the coat off, Miss O'Brien. The last thing I need is for you to get an inflammation of the lungs.'

'I am much hardier than that…my lord,' she added.

'And stop ''my lording'' me. Call me Ravensford.' He slanted her a cool smile. 'All my acquaintances do.'

Instead of responding, she gingerly slid his coat off. It dripped water and mud on the floor.

A knock preceded the door opening and a serving woman entering. 'The landlord sent me to fetch your coat, my lord.'

'Thank you,' he said. 'And please send someone

to get Miss O'Brien's cape from the coach. It will never dry there and will need cleaning.'

'Yes, my lord,' the woman said, taking the coat from Mary Margaret's hands and bundling it up. 'I will be right back to mop up this mess.'

'If you will bring the mop I will do it,' Mary Margaret volunteered, feeling badly about the puddle.

The woman gaped at her. Ravensford scowled.

'That is…I am used to cleaning up.' She knew she was making matters worse, but the words continued to tumble from her mouth.

'Why don't you show Miss O'Brien to her room? Her portmanteau should be there by now and she can change.'

The servant cast him a grateful glance. Mary Margaret realised her offer to mop the floor had made the woman feel awkward. Chagrined, she clamped down on any other words and followed the maid up a narrow flight of stairs to a small corner room. It was neat and clean with a single bed and wash stand. Her portmanteau was on the bed.

The woman left before Mary Margaret could thank her. Just as well. She would not have known what to say.

Half an hour later, she had struggled out of her wet clothing and donned dry ones. The lukewarm water in the wash bowl was brown from dirt, but she felt much better. Hunger rumbled in her stomach. Indecision kept her stationary.

Surely she was not supposed to join the Earl for supper. Which left the public room. The idea of going down among a group of men she did not know was daunting. But not so much as the thought of spending her small hoard of coins. The money was only for an emergency. She did not have enough to spend on anything else if she was going to take Emily away at the end of the quarter.

She sighed. Hungry as she was, she had been hungrier before and lived. She crossed to the bed and sat down. Exhaustion moved through her.

A knock on the door startled her.

The servant stuck her head in and said, 'His lordship be waitin' for you.'

Hunger warred with caution. Hunger won.

Minutes later, Mary Margaret entered the private room and was assailed by the smell of mutton and gravy. Her stomach growled.

'Not a second too soon,' Ravensford said with a grin. 'Have a seat, Miss O'Brien. We will eat and then we will discuss your habit of disobeying me.'

Her pleasure died. She turned to leave, knowing

that eating would only make her uncomfortable now.

'I believe I told you to sit down,' Ravensford said in a dangerously calm voice.

Mary Margaret looked back at him. His mouth was a thin line. His hands paused in the act of carving the leg of mutton. Things were going from bad to worse.

'Thank you, my lord, but I am not as hungry as I thought.' Her stomach chose that moment to put the lie to her words.

'And I am not accustomed to people disregarding my instructions, Miss O'Brien. That is the crux of this situation.'

She straightened her shoulders.

He placed a large slice of mutton on a plate that would have been hers and followed it with vegetables and gravy. Her mouth watered.

'When I tell you to do something,' he said, fixing his own plate, 'I mean for you to do exactly that. This afternoon when I told you to get back in the coach, I did so for a reason.' He took his seat, pointing toward hers with his fork. 'You got out with good intentions. I am sure you meant to lighten the load. What you really did was make the other men feel embarrassed. It is their job to take care of such situations and having a female expose herself to weather such as that made them feel even worse than they already did that the coach had hit a hole. Particularly John Coachman, and he already felt bad enough. It was much kinder for you to remain in the carriage.'

Her attention left the food and focussed on him. 'I had not thought of it that way. I had only meant to help.'

'So, when I tell you to do something, Miss O'Brien, believe that I know best.'

His autocratic manner was irritating, but she recognised the validity of his words.

'Now, please be seated. The food is getting cold.'

She did as he bade. She had thought herself no longer hungry, but the instant the food touched her tongue she was ravenous. She was nearly through when he offered her tea.

'Thank you, my lord,' she murmured, realising too late that he intended to pour for her. 'I should be doing that.'

'So you should.' He shifted the teapot, cream and sugar to her side. 'And I believe I told you to call me Ravensford.'

She stopped putting cream into her tea. 'I know, but your mother would be scandalised.'

He grinned, looking like a small boy who has pulled a prank. She could see the charm he was famous for glinting in his green eyes.

'Yes, she would be, but she isn't here.'

A picture of an irate Countess formed in Mary Margaret's mind. She smiled. 'I will try, my— Ravensford.'

'That's the way.'

He poured himself a drink and lounged back in his chair. He watched her over the rim of the glass. Mary Margaret felt like a bug pinned to a mat for someone's pleasure.

'I am very tired, m— Ravensford. And I am sure that tomorrow will be an early day. Do you mind if I go to bed?'

His scrutiny intensified. The angle of his cheek and jaw sharpened. 'Yes, I would mind, Miss O'Brien, but I will allow it. The last thing I want is for you to become exhausted before we even reach London.'

Feeling like the fox fleeing the hounds, Mary Margaret jumped up, nearly spilling her half-drunk tea. 'Thank you.'

She scurried to the door, only to find the Earl there. His large frame blocked her exit. She gazed up at him, trying to ignore the blood pounding in her ears.

He caught her chin in his well-shaped hand and rubbed his thumb back and forth over the tiny cleft below her bottom lip. She was unable to look away. He could do anything to her and she doubted that she would be able or even willing to say him nay. She gulped hard, her eyes wide.

'You are tired,' he murmured. 'I hope your bed is soft and to your satisfaction. If not, I will have you given another room.'

She did not know what to say. His solicitousness was unexpected and inappropriate. Yet a glow of warmth started in her stomach and spread. No one since her parents had cared for her like this.

'I will be fine, my lord,' she managed to mumble.

He stroked her chin one last time and let her go. Stepping away, he said, 'Ravensford. And remember, if the bed keeps you awake, I will see that something is done.'

She nodded and backed out of the door, never once taking her attention off him. Any second she half expected him to take her in his arms. They would both regret that later. So she watched him until the door closed behind her.

Only once she was safe in her room did she berate herself for over-dramatising the situation. The Earl was only interested in her comfort. If she arrived in London too tired to do what must be done to the house, then the burden would fall to him. Naturally he did not want that to happen.

But there was the caress.

She shivered beneath the thick covers. Why had

he touched her and looked at her as though he wanted to devour her? He could not be attracted to her. Surely not.

Her fingers plucked at the bedcover, finding a feather and pulling it out. What if he were interested in her? She could never be a man's mistress and he would never offer marriage. A hollowness settled in her chest.

She fell asleep, telling herself the Earl was only being considerate. She could not, would not let herself think his behaviour was for any other reason. To do so would be insane.

Downstairs Ravensford finished his drink. He wondered what hold the man in the library had over Miss O'Brien. She was a very attractive woman and well educated. While he had been angry at her leaving the carriage earlier, he had also admired her desire to be helpful. Most—no, *all* the women of his acquaintance would have stayed huddled warm and dry in the vehicle, never thinking about the servants outside in the cold and wet. She had qualities that he valued.

He templed his fingers and gazed unseeing at the fire as he brought his focus back to the problem. It did not matter that he was beginning to like her. His goal was to find out who her accomplice was and to keep them from being successful.

If seeing to her comfort did not win her trust, he could seduce her. Women always talked to their lovers. A drastic measure, but so was her plan to steal from his parent.

The idea was instantly gratifying, something he would not have thought possible. Never in his entire life had he set out to cold-bloodedly seduce a woman. He hoped he would not have to do so now—or so he told himself. It did not sit well with his idea of honour, even as the idea made his blood pool in areas best ignored.

They started early. The sun shone brightly, already drying some of the smaller puddles on the road. Mary Margaret had not slept well. She refused to breakfast with the Earl. She was not hungry and it was not proper. She had done so last night, but that did not mean she intended to continue doing so.

A brisk breeze swept across the coaching yard as she made her way to the carriage, carefully stepping around mud puddles. She was glad to have her cape back, clean and dry.

Reaching the carriage, her gaze still on the ground, she saw a pair of shining Hessians. She licked suddenly dry lips and looked up to meet Ravensford's gaze.

'Are you thirsty, Miss O'Brien? There is lemonade and hot chocolate in the carriage.' A smile tugged at one corner of his mouth.

'No, thank you. Whatever gave you that idea?'

His smile widened to a wolfish grin. 'The way you licked your lips. And you did not join me for breakfast.'

Did she detect a trace of irritation in his voice? He still smiled at her, but the showing of teeth resembled that of a large predator.

'No, I am not hungry, either.'

She looked away and started up the carriage steps. His hand caught her elbow and she halted, one foot still on the ground.

'I took the liberty of having the proprietor pack biscuits and ham for you to have later.'

She looked over her shoulder at him. Why was he doing this? She was nobody to him. He should be ignoring her.

'Thank you,' she muttered.

Hastily, before he could say or do anything else, she scampered into the coach. His hand fell away from her elbow and she breathed a sigh of relief, or so she told herself. As yesterday, she found blankets and hot stones. He was doing everything to make this journey as comfortable for her as possible. She did not understand any of this. Nor did she want it. She might have to steal from his mother if she could find no other way to save Emily and Annie.

Nervous melancholy gripped her. Somehow she had to outsmart Thomas. To escape her thoughts, she settled herself in the blankets and tried to sleep. She was exhausted and soon drifted off.

She woke with a start when the carriage jolted to a stop. Strands of hair had come loose from her chignon and she pushed them behind her ears, curious to find out what had made them stop. Peering out the window, she saw the outriders digging dirt and placing it in a large hole directly in front of the carriage.

Ravensford came over. 'They are filling any areas that might cause us to break an axle or become stuck. The last thing we need is a repeat of yesterday.'

'How clever.'

Ravensford gave her a scrutinising look. 'Have you never travelled?'

She shook her head. 'People of my station do not go far from home, my lord.'

He had the grace to look nonplussed. 'Forgive me. I didn't think.' He glanced at the men who still worked. 'Are you finding everything to your satisfaction?'

She was grateful he had changed the subject although this new one was not much more comfortable for her. 'You do too much, my lord. I don't need all of these luxuries.'

She could feel his gaze on her, giving her the sensation that the sun burned down on her exposed skin. Never had a man made her this aware of her senses.

'I already explained why you must arrive in London ready to work.'

'Yes, you did. I don't need all of this to do so. I come of hardy farmer stock.'

'You don't look it,' he murmured, his voice low and caressing and creamy. 'You look as fragile as an orchid and just as exotic.'

She gaped at him, not able to look away any longer. The intensity of his perusal seared to her toes. Confusion held her still. What was he doing?

She jumped to the first conclusion that came to mind and blurted, 'I won't become your mistress.' Instantly embarrassment overwhelmed her. 'That is—oh, dear. I didn't...I don't...'

He watched her, a gleam in his eye. 'Don't worry, Miss O'Brien, I have not asked you.'

The blush that had mounted her cheeks turned to flames. Not even a cool breeze could ease the heat that consumed her. Without considering how rude it would seem, she fell back into the coach and pulled the curtain over the window. She heard Ravensford chuckle softly.

Mortification made her stomach churn. She was such a fool.

Thankfully he did not join her for the rest of the journey. If he had, she would have had to jump out the other side of the carriage. His presence would have been too much to bear. What was she going to do for the rest of the journey? She would not be able to avoid him unless he wanted her to.

Agitation still held her when the carriage finally stopped and the scent of salt water greeted her. Impatient and not wanting Ravensford to open the door for her as he had got into the habit of doing, she opened the door herself and jumped out. She narrowly missed a puddle.

They were at a quay. At the end of the pier floated a sleek ship, probably Ravensford's. He probably called it a yacht.

'We'll be boarding immediately,' Ravensford said, coming up behind her and putting his hand to her elbow.

She had not heard him and it was all she could do not to jump. Her embarrassment rushed back so that she barely felt his fingers on her sleeve.

'I've never sailed before,' she said, not wanting to come anywhere near their last exchange of words.

He smiled down at her. 'You'll enjoy it.'

She let go a sigh of relief. He seemed focussed on sailing. She looked up at him, noting the sparkle in his eyes. 'You must like it.'

'I do.'

His valet came up. 'My lord, be careful. The mud will dirty your Hessians.'

'I shall endeavor to be careful,' Ravensford replied with a look on his face that Mary Margaret was sure hid amused resignation.

With that reassurance, the valet continued on his way, ordering the servant carrying the Earl's trunk to tread cautiously. 'Don't, whatever you do, Tom, drop that in water. That trunk is made of the finest leather.'

Mary Margaret watched the procession, amazed that someone could spend his entire life focussing on another person's clothes.

'Why so glum?' Ravensford asked.

She answered without thinking. 'That poor man is obsessed with your clothing. How boring his life must be.'

'Why do you think that?'

She glanced at him to see if he was having fun with her, but he seemed to be seriously waiting for her reply. 'Because there is so much more to life, and so much of it more important than what one wears.'

'Have you heard of Beau Brummel?'

'Who has not? I find his fixation with fashion to be very shallow.'

As they talked, the Earl continued to steer her toward the end of the pier. Up close the yacht was impressive. A gangplank connected it to land, bobbing with each wave. Mary Margaret gulped. She was not sure this was a safe means of travel. Still, at Ravensford's urging, she stepped forward.

It was worse than she had imagined. Her feet seemed to move without her volition and she was sure that if Ravensford released her elbow she would pitch over the side and into the water.

'Captain, please show Miss O'Brien to the guest cabin and see that she had everything she needs.'

'Yes, my lord.'

Mary Margaret turned to Ravensford. 'Thank you.'

He smiled at her, his eyes dancing in his unfashionably tanned face. The sun buffed his hair into strands of copper.

'I will expect to see you for lunch. It will be served on the deck under that canopy.' He pointed to a bright red and white covering that shaded a small table and several cushions.

Joining him for anything was the last thing she wanted when her knees threatened to melt under her every time he looked at her. But she had no polite refusal.

'As you wish,' she murmured.

Two hours later, she lay prostrate in the double-sized bed of her cabin. Sweat beaded her forehead and upper lip and her stomach buckled with each rise of the boat. Mary Margaret thought she had never felt worse.

'Miss.' The cabin boy's voice penetrated the closed door. 'His lordship requests your presence.'

She mumbled something.

'Pardon?'

'I…I cannot,' Mary Margaret managed to get out. 'I…am not…feeling…well.'

What seemed like an eternity later, the door opened. It was all she could do to force her eyes open. Ravensford entered without permission. He took one look at her and went to the wash basin where he dipped a cloth into the tepid water.

'Why did you not tell someone?' he demanded, squatting down by the bunk and wiping her forehead.

'I…did.' He raised one bronzed brow. She took a deep breath and stated defiantly, 'I told the…boy who…knocked. Ask him.'

Indignation at his refusal to believe gave her the

strength to grab the cloth from his hand. She wadded it up and pressed it to her mouth.

He frowned. 'Why didn't you tell me you get seasick?'

She squeezed the cloth until her knuckles turned white. 'If I had known I would have said something. Besides—' she fought the nausea down '—how else would I get to England?'

'True.' He rose on legs long accustomed to ships. 'I will be back in a moment.'

Mary Margaret stifled a moan. The last thing she wanted was to have him near her. She knew she was not a pretty woman and being sick did nothing to enhance what looks she had. Nor did she want him being around if she lost control of her stomach. She could think of nothing more humiliating.

With a groan she rolled to her side, facing the wall, and curled into a tight knot. Surely she could survive until they reached land.

The ship lurched, or so it seemed to her heightened nerves, and she wrapped her arms around her middle. At the same time, the door opened.

'Here, I've brought something for your nausea.'

The Earl's deep voice would have been arresting any other time. She turned her head just enough to look balefully up at him.

'Unless it is poison,' she muttered, closing her

eyes so as not to see the rocking cabin, 'there is nothing you can do to help.'

'Keep your eyes open and focus on something.'

Instead of answering, she curled up tighter, wishing he would go away. His hand on her shoulder shocked and angered her.

'For pity's sake, go away and let me suffer in private.' She heard him chuckle, and her wrath grew. 'How would you like to have someone bothering you when you wanted to die?'

'I tried to shoot my benefactor,' he said, all the humour gone.

'What?' She rolled on to her back to see his face.

His smile was twisted. 'It was after Salamanca.' His eyes took on a faraway look, but only for a moment. 'Now, drink this. Stevens prepared it. He claims it has ginger root and will do wonders.'

'Ginger root.' She reached with trembling hands for the mug. 'My mother would give us ginger root in warm water when we had stomach aches. It always worked.'

'Good.'

He kept hold of the mug, his fingers warm against her own. Part of her was glad. She shook so badly that without his help she would likely spill the contents. Still, some of the contents dribbled down her chin.

'You should be sitting up more.'

He took the cup from her, set it down on a table with rails to keep the cup from sliding off, and turned back to her. While he did that, she man-oeuvred herself into a semi-sitting position.

'I would have helped,' he said.

Which was the last thing she wanted. Even as sick as she felt, his touch still disturbed her in ways she did not want to experience.

'Thank you, but I can manage on my own. It should not be long before the ginger settles my stomach.'

He studied her dispassionately.

Mary Margaret felt even more dishevelled and grimy than before. Unconsciously she raised one hand to smooth her tangled hair back from her face. Large strands had worked loose from her chignon. She had to look a fright.

His gaze intensified. 'Drink your ginger root tea and after I will brush your hair.'

Heat mounted her cheeks, receded and came back. The idea of him stroking her hair was excit-ing and tempting. She told herself that having her chignon in place would make her feel almost well. That was the reason she was so tempted to let him care for her. Nothing else. She resisted.

'After I finish the drink I will be more than able to care for myself.'

'You are as weak as a kitten.'

He put the mug to her lips and tipped it so that she had to swallow. He had moved so quickly and she had been thinking about his fingers in her hair that she was caught unawares and more of the liquid dribbled down her chin. He kept the mug to her mouth until she finished. After he laid the empty container down he took the cloth from her unresisting hand and gently wiped the tea from her chin.

'Since you don't want me to brush your hair, I will take you on deck. Some fresh air will make all the difference.'

'I do not think I am up to being moved,' she mumbled.

'You look better already, and you will be glad you did,' he said, reaching down.

Before she knew what he was about, he had lifted her to his chest. She gasped. 'What are you doing?'

He shook his head as though she were a dense child and smiled down at her. 'What does it feel like, Miss O'Brien? I am taking you up on deck. The sea is calm and the fresh air will make the ginger work much faster.'

'But...but...'

Her mouth worked but nothing more came out.

His arms were comforting and strong. His heart beat steadily against her cheek. This was awful.

Ravensford strode to the door of her cabin and out.

Chapter Five

The cabin boy stood outside the door. When he saw the couple his mouth dropped open. Mary Margaret gave him a hesitant smile and wished herself anywhere but here.

'Put me down,' she hissed, her nausea abated by shock. 'This is not appropriate.'

Ravensford shrugged. 'This is my yacht and I shall do as I please. Right now it pleases me to take you on deck.'

'What if I lose control and…and…?'

'Vomit on me? You shan't be the first.'

He was insufferable.

The Captain was coming down the stairs when he saw them. He stopped in his tracks. 'My lord? May I be of assistance?'

Ravensford grinned at him. 'Make sure no one is coming down as I am going up.'

'Yes, sir.' The Captain retraced his steps. 'All clear, my lord.'

'Thank you.' Ravensford started up.

Mary Margaret was appalled. She should have never come on this journey, no matter what Thomas threatened. Never. She would not be able to look at anyone on this boat knowing they had seen this débâcle. They would think there was more between herself and Ravensford than that of servant and master.

She groaned and buried her face against Ravensford's chest. His heartbeat was oddly reassuring. He was a large man and held her easily, his arms surrounding her comfortably. She felt protected. She belonged in Bedlam.

'Here you are,' he murmured, setting her down.

Her feet hit the deck and she swayed. Immediately his arm was back around her waist, holding her tightly to his side. What had seemed protective just seconds before was now something entirely different. The breath caught in Mary Margaret's throat as the heat of his body penetrated their clothing. She did not know which was worse, being held in his arms or being held to the length of his body.

'I am perfectly able to stand on my own,' she finally managed to say, pushing against his chest.

He looked down at her. 'Are you sure?'

His concern took her aback. 'Yes. Quite.'

He released her. She stumbled backward and tripped over a chair that had been placed beside a table that was laden with food. She twisted around, reaching for something to hold on to. Her left ankle twisted.

'Oh,' she moaned as her left leg went out from under her.

Ravensford grabbed for her.

The last thing she wanted was for him to hold her. She had had more than she could tolerate already. She scooted away. Her hand caught something cold and hard. She realised it was the ship's railing just instants before she tumbled over it.

She hit the water with an icy splash. She sank down, her skirts pulling her deeper. Fear galvanised her. She struggled to the surface and gasped for air. She did not know how to swim. Her legs tangled in her skirts. Her arms flailed.

Ravensford watched in horror as Mary Margaret disappeared over the side of the yacht. Without even thinking, he shed his coat and boots and dived into the water. He surfaced several feet from her just in time to see her sink beneath the surface for a second time.

He dived again, kicking with all his strength. The salt water burned his eyes, but he had to keep her in sight. Mercifully he caught her. He circled

her waist with one arm and thrust upward with his
legs and free arm.

He thought his lungs would burst, but he had to
get them to the surface. Her skirts twisted around
his legs, making it next to impossible to get any
power, and added to her weight. Without a second
thought, he ripped the woollen fabric from her
body. The loss of weight made her seem nearly
buoyant. He kicked hard, sending them upward.

They popped into the air and both breathed
deeply. Ravensford trod water, one hand under
Mary Margaret's shoulders and the other moving
in circles to help keep them afloat.

'Stay calm, sweetings,' he murmured. 'Everything is fine. They will get us.'

Her large, scared eyes clung to his. She nodded,
her lips trembling.

'Breathe,' he commanded. 'Breathe.'

It was only minutes before the yacht lowered a
boat. To Ravensford, watching Mary Margaret's
pale face, it seemed like an eternity.

He felt the heat seep from his own body and
knew Mary Margaret was in worse shape. She had
been in the water longer and was slimmer. He had
to get her out of here.

'Hold on to my neck,' he ordered, rolling to his
side. Her teeth chattered and her lips were blue,
but she nodded and did as he said. 'That's my girl.'

Her wide, frightened eyes stared into his. He forced a smile and started kicking. They moved slowly toward the oncoming boat. Hands reached for them not a minute too soon.

Ravensford thrust Mary Margaret into the arms of the first seaman and pushed her into the small vessel. When she was safely on board, he followed.

She huddled on the wooden seat, a tiny, bedraggled ball. Her shoulders shook. He slid next to her and gathered her close. Using his hands, he chafed her arms.

'Are there no blankets?' he demanded, his voice harsh with worry.

'No, milord,' one of the two seamen answered, never stopping in his rowing.

Disgusted, Ravensford pulled her on to his lap. Anything to warm her chill skin. She did not protest. She did not say a thing. That, more than anything else, scared him.

'Come on, sweetings, rail at me,' he ordered, rubbing her back and arms.

Instead of speaking, she burrowed deeper into the warmth of his body. He groaned.

Finally they reached the yacht and a rope stair was lowered. There was no way he could climb it and carry Mary Margaret.

'You have to let go of me,' he murmured, stroking the hair from her face. 'You have to climb that rope.'

She looked from him to the ladder. Her jaw clenched, and he felt her tremble. But she rose from his lap and gripped the rope. Slowly, she climbed.

He followed closely behind, ready to catch her if she slipped. Only now that she was nearly safe did Ravensford notice her clothing. He had ripped her skirts away so that only her pantaloons remained. They were translucent.

He swallowed hard.

Her derrière swelled enticingly against the white fabric. Her hips flared out into shapely thighs.

He climbed up behind her, noticing that the Captain was trying to keep his gaze averted from Mary Margaret's near nakedness. Ravensford smiled wryly. The Captain was a better man than he. He had completely given up on looking away. But that did not mean he would leave her exposed like this for everyone to see.

He grabbed his coat from the deck and wrapped it around her before lifting her and striding to the stairs. Her head fell back on his shoulder. Her face was white and her breath came in little sobs. All he wanted was to comfort her.

Minutes later, he shouldered open her cabin door

and entered, closing it behind them. He laid her gently on the bed.

Her eyes opened. 'I have never been more scared in my life,' she whispered, her lips still blue.

'And all my fault,' he said, smoothing her loose hair back from her forehead.

She smiled wanly. 'No. I am the one whose clumsiness sent me pitching over the side.'

He took his coat from her and quickly wrapped a blanket around her, careful to keep his gaze averted. 'If I had not insisted on taking you on deck, it would have never happened.'

Her eyes closed and she sank back into the pillow.

He gazed at her, unable to resist the memory of her nearly naked in his arms. Her full, rounded breasts pressed against his chest, their tips rosy and taut from cold as they strained against the thin fabric of her chemise. Her rounded hips and slender thighs snuggled into his loins. His body tightened painfully. He closed his eyes, knowing that he could not stop himself from picturing her naked and in his bed.

Her hand on his arm drew his awareness. He took a deep breath and looked at her.

Her black brows were drawn in worry. 'Are you getting sick, my lord? You look in pain.'

He groaned. Seducing her and getting her to tell

him everything about the plan to steal from his mother was supposed to be a last resort if he could not win her trust. Picturing her naked in his bed was not going to accomplish his goal.

He forced himself to speak clearly instead of rasping like someone pushed to his physical limit. 'I am fine, Miss O'Brien. You are the one who is not feeling well.'

He straightened and moved away. Still, the outline of her body under the blanket did things to him that made his skin-hugging wet pantaloons even tighter.

'I am not seasick any more,' she said, a hint of amusement in her voice.

The deep purr of her voice slid along his nerves, adding to his discomfort. He had to get out of here or he would ravish her—immediately, without any regard for what she wanted.

'I will get Stevens, Miss O'Brien. He will have just the thing to keep you from getting a fever.'

He strode from the room, shutting the cabin door firmly behind himself. For long moments he stood with his back to the wall, taking deep breaths and trying to tame his body. It was no use. Every time he saw her he was going to see the way she looked lying in that bed, her luscious figure as good as bare.

'My lord,' Stevens said, coming up the tiny hall-way, 'are you ill?'

He released a bark of laughter. Ill with desire and there was only one cure for that. 'No, Stevens, but I fear Miss O'Brien might become so if she is not given one of your possets.'

The valet became brisk. 'Tut, tut. We cannot have that, my lord. The Countess's maid told me the responsibility Miss O'Brien will have in London. There is no time for the young woman to be sick.'

'Right you are,' Ravensford managed. 'No time at all.'

'You go change, my lord.' Stevens gave his master an appalled look. 'That is—'

'I can take my own clothes off and put others on,' Ravensford said. 'The results won't be as polished as when you assist me, but I will be decent.'

His thoughts flicked again to Mary Margaret. What would it be like to have her undress him? He could not think of that right now.

'Of course, my lord. Then I shall take care of Miss O'Brien. Do not worry about a thing.'

Only my sanity, Ravensford thought, as he watched Stevens enter Miss O'Brien's cabin. No woman had ever aroused him this quickly and completely. His reaction was as disconcerting as it was pleasurable.

Nor had any woman aroused his protective instincts as she had. He could tell himself all he wanted that he was concerned because her brush with death had been his fault, but he knew that was only part of it. Mary Margaret O'Brien was beginning to matter to him.

Mary Margaret tugged at her hair with a brush. They were docking any moment now and her hair was still damp. If she put it in a chignon, it would never dry. If she wore it loose, she would look like a doxy.

And her dress. She wore her second-best dress. Her travelling outfit was at the bottom of the sea. Her chemise and pantaloons were stiff from salt and would have to wait until they stopped for the night before she could properly wash them. Everything was a mess.

But she was not seasick. That was a great comfort.

A knock on her door preceded the Earl's voice. 'Miss O'Brien, we are docked and will be unloading immediately. We have a ways to go before we reach tonight's inn.'

She jumped up, twisting her hair into a knot. Heat suffused her entire body. Only when she had changed clothes had she realised that her pantaloons and chemise might as well not have existed

for all the cover they had given her. Ravensford
had seen every inch of her as though she had been
naked. And so had the crew. The last thing she
wanted was the Earl in this cabin.

'I am ready, my lord,' she said hurriedly, breathlessly. 'I will be out.'

'Good. I will meet you on deck in five minutes.'

'Yes, my lord.'

'Ravensford.'

She heard him move away. What had he thought
about her dishabille? Had it disgusted him that she
had not even realised her exposure and so had not
shown any modesty? She moaned. Nor had she
thanked him for saving her life.

With a groan she realised that one hand still held
her hair twisted into a knot on her neck. She
quickly jabbed several pins into the thick tresses
until they were secure. She would worry about drying her hair later. As it was, the strands smelled of
sea water and salt. She would have to wash it when
they got to the inn. Until then, there was nothing
else she could do.

This trip was horrible. Her only consolation was
that it could not possibly get worse.

She was wrong. Having the gaze of every crew
member watching her walk the gangplank was ex-
cruciating. The only thing that got her through the
gauntlet was pride. Ravensford waited for her.

His eyes smouldered as she approached him. His gaze swept over her. She remembered all too clearly how she had looked when she rose from the bunk to change and caught sight of herself in the mirror. He had seen her all but naked.

Embarrassment flooded her cheeks.

'You look none the worse for your ducking,' he said, extending his arm.

She sighed and considered walking past him, but that would only add to the speculation so rampant in the faces of the men watching them. She stopped and laid her fingers lightly on his arm, nearly wincing from the heat he radiated.

'I owe you a great debt, my lord.'

He frowned. 'You are a stubborn woman. How many times must I order you to call me Ravensford?'

She quirked one brow at him, and instantly regretted it. His smile could charm the chemise off a lady of Quality, let alone someone as susceptible to him as she was.

'I would berate you over not using my name,' he murmured so no one else could hear, 'but it would do no good.'

She did not answer, thinking herself lucky they were in public and the heat in his gaze could not be directed at her in a more physical manner. She was weak enough to succumb.

'Let me help you up,' he said, stopping and putting his large, strong hands around her waist.

Totally immersed in what she imaged his kiss would be like, Mary Margaret was taken by surprise. 'Wha...what are you doing?' she babbled.

He smiled down at her. 'Lifting you into my phaeton.'

She looked up and gulped. He was too close and the contraption he wanted to put her into was too high. She gripped one of his forearms with each hand and pushed him until he released her. She stepped back.

Raised in the country, Mary Margaret had never seen a carriage like the one before her. It was high off the ground, with room for two only. The finish was a glossy hunter green with thin black lines outlining the curves. Two prancing chestnuts stood impatiently in the traces, a young boy in the Earl's livery holding them in place. Altogether a dangerous means of transportation.

'What kind of vehicle is this?'

He laughed. 'This is a high-perch phaeton. The fastest carriage on the roads.'

'And the most deadly,' she said flatly.

He sobered instantly. 'Not with the right driver.'

She stepped away, not wanting to be any closer to the thing than she had to be. 'Isn't there another

carriage I can ride in? The baggage must be somewhere. I will go with it. 'Tis only proper.'

He caught her as she turned away. 'I am considered a fair hand with the ribbons, Miss O'Brien.
I won't tip you into a ditch.'

''Is lordship be a prime member o' the Four-in-
'and Club, miss,' the young boy said proudly.

Ravensford smiled at the lad. 'Thank you, Peter.'

'Whatever the Four-in-Hand Club is,' Mary
Margaret muttered.

Scandalised, the youth spoke up again. ''It be a
group of swells what knows how to 'andle the ribbons like no others. 'Is lordship is the best.'

'Thank you again, Peter,' Ravensford said. 'I
think I can deal with this on my own now.'

The lad flushed.

'I can get you to the inn much quicker this way,
Miss O'Brien. You can eat and be in bed by the
time the baggage carriage reaches the inn. Think
about how nice it will be to have a full stomach
and a nice soft bed that does not move.'

She eyed him. He had a point. Exhaustion ate
at her and her stomach fussed at her. She looked
back at the phaeton.

'I promise not to spill you,' Ravensford said as
though reading her mind.

'Well…'

'Up with you, then,' he said.

Before she realised what he intended, his hands were around her waist and lifting her up. It was either step into the carriage or continue to be held aloft by him. Entering the phaeton was more dignified and less intimate than his hands wrapped around her waist.

She sat down gingerly, feeling the carriage sway slightly. When Ravensford climbed in, the vehicle bounced on well-sprung wheels. The breath caught in her throat. Then he sat beside her, and she scooted to the very edge of the seat, only to look down. The ground seemed a long way away.

She sighed.

'I won't bite,' he said, a wicked grin belying his words.

Before she could think of a suitable reply, Stevens hurried up with a blanket. 'This is for Miss O'Brien,' he said, handing it to her. 'It would not do for you to catch an inflammation, miss, after your ducking.'

She took the warm wool covering. 'Thank you, Stevens. This will be very nice.'

Ravensford took the blanket from her without asking and spread it over her lap and legs. His gloved fingers moved over her thighs with a sureness that made the breath catch in her throat. Seconds before she had worried about falling out and breaking her neck. Now she knew the greater danger was sitting so closely to the Earl.

They could travel as fast as the wind and it would still be too slow for her peace of mind and body.

Chapter Six

The carriage came to a sudden halt and Mary Margaret jolted awake, her cheek bumping against something hard and unyielding. Dazed, she pummelled whatever her head had been resting on.

'That is my shoulder, if you don't mind,' a deep voice drawled.

Memory came back in a mortifying rush. She was in the Earl's high-perch phaeton which he had stored here in England while he had been in Ireland. The baggage carriage he had hired was somewhere behind them.

'Pardon me, my lord.' She sat up and straightened her bonnet, which had fallen to one side of her head.

'Let me do that.' He angled around after handing the reins to his tiger.

'Thank you, but I can manage.' The last thing

she wanted was for him to touch her. He had already had his hands on her more than enough these last twenty-four hours.

He ignored her—as usual.

He carefully set the bonnet to rights, leaning back to get a better look. He shifted it slightly to one side. She glared at him. He smiled lazily. His eyes held hers captive as his fingers dropped to the ribbons tied under her chin. He undid the knotted bow and retied the silk into a rakish bow just under her right ear.

'There. A lady's maid could not have done better.'

The urge to say something scathing nearly overwhelmed her good sense. But she managed not to make a difficult moment more so.

'Thank you again,' she muttered, trying hard to keep her resentment from coming out.

He jumped abruptly from the carriage and held an imperious hand up to her. Another touch. She sighed. The only way to stop this was to grit her teeth and do what was necessary so that she could get to her room.

He smiled up at her, the emotion reaching his eyes and making the corners crinkle. Somehow he knew his touch bothered her. She never had been good at hiding her feelings.

'Come along. You need some food and rest.'

Her gaze skittered away from his. His voice had been deep and dark, hinting at things she only barely understood and definitely did not want to delve into. Still, her heart pounded and her skin tingled when she put her fingers in his. He helped her down, continuing to hold her hand longer than was necessary.

'Thank you,' she murmured. Then added with some asperity, 'I can walk on my own, just not on a boat.'

Even to her own ears her words had been breathy and disturbed. No wonder he continued to gaze at her, his fingers wrapped firmly around her skin. Was it her imagination, or was his face closer? Her heart skipped a beat.

He laughed. 'I hope never to have such an experience again. You scared ten years off my life.'

A strange fluttering started in her stomach. 'Well, I can assure you that the ducking did not prolong mine any.'

Belatedly, she realised that he still held her hand. She pulled but, instead of releasing her, he tucked her fingers into the crook of his elbow. His attentions were too marked. She caught one of the outriders watching with a smirk on his face. She looked away.

'I have bespoken dinner and rooms. There should be no delays before you seek your bed.'

She started shivering. He took off his many-caped great coat and wrapped it around her.

'Come,' he said, leading her to the front door.

She followed without protest, too shocked by his behaviour to do anything else. He treated her as though she was a lady of Quality and someone whose comfort he cared about. He made her feel safe.

She stumbled inside, Ravensford's arm supporting her. The landlord stood eyeing them. His gaze went from her to the Earl.

'My lord,' the owner said, rushing forward. 'Your rooms are ready and supper will be served immediately. I kept the parlour for you.'

Ravensford nodded his head. 'Thank you, John. Please show Miss O'Brien to her room so she can change into dry clothes.'

The landlord nodded, casting a scandalised look at Mary Margaret. 'Will your man be bringing in the luggage, my lord?'

Ravensford nodded. 'I will wait for you, Miss O'Brien, before starting supper.'

Mary Margaret felt dazed. Too much too fast. With fingers numb from nerves, she pulled the Earl's coat off and handed it to him.

'I would be happy with toast and butter and a pot of hot tea in my room.'

'I have bespoken dinner, Miss O'Brien, and I would like your company.'

Aware of the landlord watching them, she nodded. 'As you wish, my lord.'

'I will expect you as soon as you have freshened up.'

He turned and strode back to the coach yard. He had not been this high-handed with his mother. When she had requested something, he had agreed. Did he treat all other women this way, or only her?

'This way, miss,' the landlord said, breaking into her thoughts.

She followed him up a flight of stairs. He paused and opened a door.

'His lordship's room is across the hall.'

She glanced sharply at the man, wondering if there was more to his words. His countenance was bland.

'Thank you.'

'Dinner will be served downstairs, in the room next to the commons.'

'Thank you,' she said again as she slipped inside.

She shut the door slowly, giving the landlord time to back away. Immediately there was a knock. This time it was one of the Earl's servants, delivering her portmanteau.

'Thank you,' she said once again, smiling at the man.

When she was finally alone, she turned to view her room—and froze. This had to be one of the best, if not the best, available. A large four-poster bed took pride of place with a massive wardrobe and elaborate nightstand grouped around it. The fire was ablaze with two chairs pulled cosily close. Flowers in muted colours rioted beneath her feet.

She shook her head in amazement.

Another knock brought a sigh of exasperation. Who was it this time? She opened the door to a bobbing maid.

'His lordship ordered a bath.'

Another maid appeared, lugging a hip tub. Before Mary Margaret could protest, everything was arranged and the maids were gone. She was cold and grimy and the steaming water was an invitation she could not resist. It felt so good to get the salt out of her hair.

She was clean, warm in her second-best dress and half-asleep when the summons came. The maid who had brought the tub said, 'His lordship sent me to escort you to his private dining room, miss.'

Mary Margaret's first inclination was to plead exhaustion. She could not be so rude. Ravensford had taken every care for her comfort, the least she could do was go down and thank him. She did not have to stay. With that self-deluding thought, she followed the maid.

The maid left her at the door.

Mary Margaret took a deep breath and told herself that the tightness in her chest was due to the soaking she had taken earlier. The same for her shaking fingers. Resolutely, she knocked. His deep baritone bid her enter and the air went out of her lungs.

She chided herself for overreacting. He was her employer. If he ever found out that the sound of his voice made her stomach feel like lightning was striking it, he would laugh.

In one fluid motion she turned the handle and entered. He stood near the fire, one forearm resting on the mantel, one booted foot propped on the andiron. His brown jacket fit his lean form loosely. The collar of his white shirt was open. His casualness accentuated the rugged lines of his face.

Her pulse jumped.

To hide the delight she felt, Mary Margaret bobbed a curtsy and averted her face so that she talked to the fire. 'Thank you for everything, my lord. You have been more than kind. I must return to my room now.'

His low chuckle was like velvet stroking her

skin, but his voice was firm. 'It's Ravensford and you will eat something first.'

'I'm not hungry.' She backed up. The room was suddenly overly hot.

He smiled and a dimple peeked out of his left cheek, softening the harsh lines of his jaw. She wondered if he knew how devastating his smile was. Probably.

'Truly, I am more tired than hungry. But I thank you for offering.'

He lifted one brow. 'Another argument over dinner, Miss O'Brien? This becomes boring.'

She lifted her chin. 'Then you will not wish my company, my lord.'

He laughed. 'Very good, but not good enough. Sit down and be done with this.'

He moved to the table placed just in front of the fire and lifted the cover off one of the dishes. The aroma of roast beef filled the room, making her stomach growl. Lunch had been a long time ago. She blushed at the indelicacy.

He eyed her knowingly. 'Come, eat some of this and then I promise to let you go.'

He was right, she needed to eat. She sank into the chair he had indicated.

He carved a large piece of beef and set it on a plate, added some potatoes and peas, and set it all in front of her. Next he handed her the tea and let her lace it with cream and sugar. He poured himself an amber-coloured liquid with a smoky scent.

He sat after loading his plate with twice what he had put on hers. Neither spoke much for a while.

Ravensford watched her eat with dainty dispatch. He could almost image delicate whiskers twitching. When her pointed pink tongue darted out to lick a drop of tea from her lip his gut clenched. Pictures of her lying practically naked in the bunk raged through his mind. Blood pounded in his ears. He took a deep breath. He wondered if she knew how arousing she was. Perhaps not.

She looked up and caught him looking at her. He smiled.

'You eat like a cat, delicately and focussed,' he said.

She laid her fork and knife down. He watched her magnificent bosom swell as she watched him. He knew she wanted to say something, probably not complimentary, but was restraining herself.

After a long pause, she said, 'My lord, why are you treating me like this? I am not Quality, nor am I your responsibility.'

He leaned back in his chair, finished with his food even though half of it still remained on his plate. He sipped his whiskey and eyed her over the glass rim. Why was he treating her this way?

He had set out to gain her trust, but that did not

mean he had to treat her like a prized companion or force his presence on her when she did not want it. Nor did he have to be the one to dive in to save her. Any one of his sailors could have done so. Just as Stevens could have nursed her through her seasickness from the beginning.

Why was he doing this?

The answer was startling, although he instantly realised it should not be. His reaction to her was stronger than he'd had to any other woman. His body was like an adolescent around her, aroused and aching all the time.

'Be my mistress. I will pay you well and you will no longer have to endure my mother's slights.'

She dropped the cup of tea she had just lifted to her lips. It hit the table with a thump, sending scalding tea all over the cloth. Neither one paid it any mind.

'You jest, and very cruelly,' she said.

Amazed at his bluntness, Ravensford shook his head slowly. 'No, I don't believe I do, Miss O'Brien—Mary Margaret. In fact, I have never been so serious about asking a woman to become my mistress as I am now.'

Her bosom heaved in agitation and her eyes flashed anger. Even knowing she was about to refuse him, he enjoyed the show. She was not a traditional beauty, but she appealed very much to him.

She licked her lips and his loins tightened. He downed the whiskey, wondering if it would numb his nether parts. He could only try, for it was obvious she was not going to help him in that area.

She stormed to her feet. 'I am not…not a loose woman. I might not be your equal, my lord, but that does not make me someone you can take advantage of so cavalierly.'

He stood, admiring the way fury put colour into her high cheeks and brought a flutter to her breasts. How he wanted her.

'My apologies, Miss O'Brien. It was my baser self speaking.' He gave her a roguish grin. 'But should you change your mind, don't hesitate to tell me.'

She stalked to the door. Turning, she asked, 'May I be excused?'

Sarcasm was something he had not heard in her throaty voice before. He did not like hearing it now, but he deserved it. He had overstepped the bounds of propriety.

He bowed her from the room, wondering how he was going to survive the rest of the journey in such close proximity to her.

It was just as well that she had refused him. She

was a potential thief, not a potential mistress—no matter what his body said.

Mary Margaret woke before the sun was up. She sat up, only to fall back on to the pillows. Her head felt like a herd of sheep pounded through it. Her throat hurt. Her heart ached.

She moaned.

She did not know which felt worse, her body or her spirit. Just moving was an effort, but remembering last night was a nightmare. Ravensford had asked her to be his mistress and she had turned him down. Shame warred with anger and regret with relief.

She rolled to her side, ignoring the tightness in her chest, and buried her face in the pillow. The linens were still damp from her tears of last night. Exhaustion was the only reason she had been able to sleep, and even then her dreams had been full of loss and longing.

How could she face him today? With luck, she would die of consumption and not have to. She was being a coward. Ravensford was the one who should be ashamed, not she. He was the one who had acted improperly, not she.

She flipped on to her back, fists clenched, jaw clamped. Her head protested with a sharp pain at the temples. No matter how she felt, she needed to get up. They were leaving at dawn.

She managed to dress herself. Determination held her upright when she swayed on her feet. She had survived worse. She would live through this. However, a cup of tea laced with honey and cream would be very nice.

When the maid knocked, she was ready. Carrying her portmanteau, she followed the woman downstairs. Ravensford sat in the common room and chose that moment to look up from his ham and ale.

He rose and walked to Mary Margaret, his stride loose-hipped and easy. To her jaundiced eye, he looked like nothing had occurred between them.

'Please join me,' he said, stopping just short of her, his fresh citrus scent filling her senses.

She studied him through narrowed eyes. 'No, thank you,' she said, her voice a painful rasp in her throat.

He frowned. 'You are sick. Come and have some tea and toast. I will send for Stevens to fix you another one of his possets.'

She shook her head and winced. 'I don't want anything to eat and would prefer to have my tea in the carriage.'

He took her by the arm and propelled her toward his table. She resisted the urge to dig her heels in.

When they reached the seats, she forced a false smile to her lips.

'You must not have heard me, my lord, but I prefer to take tea in the carriage.'

Ravensford gave her a tight stretch of lips. 'I know what you would prefer, but you and I have some things to discuss.'

She blanched.

'My lord,' the proprietor said, coming in through the door from the kitchen with a laden tray. 'The lady's tea is ready.'

Ravensford resumed his seat and the landlord set out the teapot, cream, sugar, cup and saucer, and a plate of scones with butter and marmalade. In spite of her sore throat, the smell of warm bread and steaming tea drew her. When the proprietor looked expectantly at her, she gave in.

'Please bring some honey,' Ravensford said, 'and see if someone can find my valet.'

The landlord hurried out on his errands.

Mary Margaret felt Ravensford's gaze as she fixed a cup of tea and a scone. When she glanced up at him, his attention was on her fingers as she broke off a piece of the pastry. His gaze followed her fingers and the scone to her mouth. A dark hunger entered his eyes, making them appear hunter green in the dim light of the room. She shivered.

His eyes met hers. 'I want you.'

His voice was deep and husky. His mouth was a grim curve of sensualness. Her stomach churned as her body went from cold to hot. The scone dropped from nerveless fingers.

'I...I told you last night, my lord,' she said, her voice a harsh whisper.

'That was last night. Tell me again,' he demanded, his gaze never leaving her face.

Her chest constricted and she felt as though she was suffocating. The room was unbearably warm. One hand fluttered to the high neckline of her dress.

'I am not that kind of woman.' She took a deep breath. 'Please stop asking me.'

His lips thinned, but he leaned back in his chair. 'My apologies,' he finally said, his voice nearly normal. 'I have never wanted a woman as I want you. I find it harder than I would have thought to take no for an answer.'

She gulped, more uncomfortable than she could remember being in a long time. Turning her face away from the intensity of his, she started to rise. One of his large, strong hands caught her wrist, keeping her sitting.

'Please don't go,' he said. 'You need the food and tea. I will leave.'

She nodded, unable to reply.

But instead of standing, he said, 'We will put this behind us—for now. You are under my protection and it was ungentlemanly of me. However...' he gave her a rueful grin '...I think it would be best if you make the rest of the journey in the baggage carriage with Stevens. You are sick and the exposure of the phaeton would not be good for you, and I am not at my best around you.'

He stood abruptly, bowed and left her.

She stared after him, nonplussed. Everything had happened so quickly and her head felt like it was packed with cotton. At least she did not have to continue travelling in the Earl's company. He was as much a temptation to her as he claimed she was to him.

Stevens said from behind her, 'Miss O'Brien, do you know where his lordship has gone? He sent for me.'

Still dazed, she turned to look at the valet. 'I don't know.'

'You have a cold,' the valet said. 'I will fix you another posset.'

Even as she murmured her thanks, he left, moving swiftly and purposefully. She knew that in a short time the posset would arrive. She wished her heart could be cured as easily as Stevens's posset intended to cure her inflammation. Right now she felt as though her world would never be the same again.

With a sigh, she drank the now-lukewarm tea.

Ravensford watched Mary Margaret climb into the baggage carriage. Even though she was bundled up as though she expected a snow storm, he could still make out the line of her hips. He shook his head in exasperation. He was like a boy still wet behind the ears where she was concerned.

Besides, he had not arranged this trip so he could seduce her—not originally. His plan was to gain her trust and get her to tell him about the plan to rob his mother. Now he would be lucky if she even spoke to him again.

He sighed and turned away from the inn window. Stevens stood patiently by the door, waiting for instructions.

'See that Miss O'Brien has every comfort,' Ravensford said, taking a full purse from his bed and giving it to the valet. 'I shall be travelling on ahead. With good weather and no problems, I can be in London within the week. You will be much slower.'

'Yes, my lord,' Stevens said, taking the money.

'I know I can count on you.'

A smile of genuine pleasure lit the valet's face before he left. Ravensford turned back to the window. He had not planned on travelling ahead, but even as he had said the words he had known they were for the best.

Mary Margaret had refused his offer of protection; the last thing she or he needed was for him to continue importuning her. Much as he desired her, his actions disgusted him. He did not believe in taking advantage of others, particularly those less fortunate than him.

So why was he so determined to have her? He did not know, but he was going to stop this stupidity once and for all. A separation was the best thing for him.

Unfortunately, she very likely agreed.

Chapter Seven

Excitement held Mary Margaret spellbound as they reached the London outskirts. Not even Steven's severe countenance could dampen her spirits. He was frowning at her because she insisted on opening the window so she could see everything better. He did not want her to have a relapse from the cool spring air.

She had not seen the Earl since he passed them on the road their first day out from the inn. She told herself it was better this way, but no amount of reasoning eased the ache in her heart. She would have never thought it possible to care for someone she barely knew, but against all logic she did.

So what if there was no excitement to her day and each hour dragged by? She was used to life's easy flow. If she was bored, then it was her own fault as her mother had so often said. When they reached the Earl's town house she would use some of her precious money to send Emily a letter. Her sister would love to hear all about London.

In order to have plenty to write about, Mary Margaret concentrated on the outside. There were people everywhere, dressed in all manner of styles. Vendors crowded the streets.

The coach slowed and she noticed that while there were still plenty of pedestrians, they were more stylish. The men resembled the Earl, the women the Countess. More phaetons and curricles passed them, all drawn by prime horseflesh. The houses were larger and more ornately decorated.

Shortly, the carriage stopped. Stevens got out without giving her a glance. She told herself that was as it should be. Still, a rebellious part of her missed the Earl's attentions.

She chided herself. Not only was she silly, she was wicked. The Earl had made his intentions clear and they were not honourable.

Gathering the skirts of her only presentable dress into one hand, she jumped out. Before her stood a house more grand than the Countess's estate in Ireland. She craned her neck to see up to the roof. Four stories, all with elegantly carved windows and cornices. The house fit her impression of Ravensford—powerful and magnificent.

Belatedly, she realised they were at the servants'

entrance. She could not image what the front looked like. An open door emitted delicious smells so she entered and found herself in the kitchen. A man speaking French and waving around a butcher's knife could only be the chef. Young boys scrambled to do his bidding, whether they understood him or not. Several girls scrubbed big copper pots.

She stood in the middle of the jumble, not knowing what to do or where to go. She had just decided to go back outside and fetch her portmanteau when a short woman stopped in front of her.

'You must be Miss O'Brien. I am Mrs Brewster, the housekeeper. Come along, now. No sense dawdling in the Frenchie's domain. Gaston fixes the best meals in London, but his temperament is volatile.' She shook her head and started off without glancing back to see if Mary Margaret followed.

Mary Margaret trailed the housekeeper's tiny, black-clad figure from the kitchen. Just past the green baize door were a narrow set of stairs. Mrs Brewster started up them. Two flights up, the housekeeper took a turn and came out on a wide landing. Delicate carpeting muffled their steps. Silver sconces with wax candles flooded the area with light. They were in the family portion of the house.

Three doors down, the housekeeper turned to face Mary Margaret. The older woman's face was narrow and lined at the mouth and eyes. Her brown hair was thick and braided tightly to her head. A delicate white cap perched properly on her crown. Her hazel eyes looked Mary Margaret over. She must have liked what she saw because she smiled.

'His lordship told me to put you here. If there is anything you'll be needing, let me know. A boy will bring your luggage up shortly. I will have a tray sent up. I am sure you are hungry and thirsty.'

Mary Margaret smiled in relief. She had been afraid that Mrs Brewster would somehow know the Earl had asked her to become his mistress. If the housekeeper did know, she was still treating Mary Margaret like a respectable lady.

'Thank you, Mrs Brewster. Thank you so much.'

The older woman smiled gently. 'I know how strange it can be your first time in London. And I know what a large task you have ahead of you. I'll do my best to help you.'

Mary Margaret blinked back tears. She was exhausted. Mrs Brewster opened the door and Mary Margaret entered, hearing it close behind her. She stood transfixed by the grandeur of the room. Surely there was some mistake.

She yanked open the door and, seeing Mrs Brewster's figure just disappearing around the corner, ran after her. 'Madam, Mrs Brewster,' she gasped when she caught up with the other woman, 'there must be some mistake. I am the Countess's companion, not a guest.'

Mrs Brewster shook her head. 'No, miss, there is not. His lordship picked the room himself.'

Mary Margaret took a step back. Oh, dear. Even after her refusal, Ravensford had continued to get her the best rooms available in the inns they stopped at, but she had thought that was just consideration and that things would return to a more normal aspect once they reached London.

'Thank you, Mrs Brewster.' She continued backing away, watching the other woman for any hint of what she felt. There was none. 'I am sorry I bothered you.'

'Quite all right, miss. I thought you might be surprised.'

There was nothing to say to that. Mary Margaret nodded and turned around. She needed privacy to come to grips with this most recent incident.

But first she had to become accustomed to her room.

It was nearly the size of her sister Emily's entire house. No wonder Thomas was so bitter if he grew up like this. He had fallen far.

Shamrock-green silk curtains were pulled back to admit the late afternoon sun. The ceiling-to-floor windows looked out on the back of the house and an Elizabethan garden and maze. A wrought-iron gazebo snuggled in one corner. She would have to explore it as soon as possible.

Under her feet was the thickest and most luxurious carpet she had ever seen. Vines and ivy dotted with delicate pink roses spread like a verdant jungle. Two Chippendale chairs, upholstered in pink-striped silk and green trim were grouped cosily around a mahogany pie table with inlaid sandalwood designs.

And then there was the huge four-poster bed with its green and pink curtains and mountainous pillows. She would be lost in it. But the Earl would not.

She flushed and buried her face in her hands. How could she think such a thing? The memory of his smouldering gaze while he waited for her reply gave her the answer. She might not want to be his mistress, but she wanted to be more to him than his mother's companion.

She took a deep breath and regained her composure. He was far above her, and she was supposed to steal from his mother.

She shook her head to clear it of the troubling thoughts and strode across the room to another door. It was a dressing room. She laughed, not a happy sound. She had three dresses to her name and a ruined cape, one pair of boots that the constant rain and mud had taken a toll on and a pair of leather slippers. She did not need this room in the least.

She shut the door with a firm hand. Still, Ravensford had been more than generous with her. She would have so much to tell Emily, and even a desk to write on, she noted. The light, fully stocked lady's desk nestled between the two windows. She sat at it and took a sheet of the Earl's embossed stationery. She dipped the quill in the ink and began.

It was dusk when she finished. A knock on the door caught her attention. Her dinner waited, as did a bath when she was finished eating. Life with the Countess had not been anything near like this.

Three weeks later, Mary Margaret wiped her brow before finishing the arrangement of a large bouquet of lilacs from the Earl's garden. The vase, overflowing with the lavender blooms, sat in the salon between two floor-to-ceiling windows that faced the front street. The town house was as ready as she could make it with the help of the entire staff. When she had been in doubt about something, the Earl's secretary had provided the needed information. Even Ravensford's valet, Stevens, approved.

The Countess and Annabell Winston were to arrive today. She waited in apprehension, hoping the

Countess would be pleased but knowing that she would find fault with something. That was how it had been in Ireland; she did not expect it to be any different here. But that was all right. She had done her best, and she had a sense of satisfaction.

'Well done, Miss O'Brien.'

She jumped. The Earl's butterscotch baritone sent shivers down her spine.

'I didn't mean to startle you.'

'I did not hear you, my lord. And thank you.' She made her hands relax at her side. 'I could not have done it without the staff and your secretary. Mr Kartchner has been invaluable.'

'I find him so. And my staff is the best in London. I am glad they could be of assistance.'

Silence fell between them. A long, awkward silence that made Mary Margaret search her brain for something, anything to say. Nothing came to mind.

'How do you find your room, Miss O'Brien?'

For some reason that was the last thing she had expected. 'Lovely. I have never seen anything so beautiful, let alone lived in something so magnificent.' She laughed nervously. 'I pinch myself every morning to make sure I am not dreaming it. I am sure that I should be on the fourth floor with the other servants.'

He frowned. 'I don't care how my mother treats you, I will treat you as you deserve.'

'Thank you, my lord.' Her voice was tight. He always made her feel awkward.

'And stop thanking me and calling me "my lord". I told you to call me Ravensford.' His eyes darkened. 'Or have you forgotten?'

She had forgotten nothing—not his order to call him Ravensford or his offer of *carte blanche*. 'Yes, m...' She caught herself. It was better to humour him. 'Ravensford.'

'Better.'

He pivoted on his heel and strode from the room, taking her by surprise. It was as though he had suddenly lost interest in their conversation. What a ninny she was to have been so totally caught up in their interaction. It was obvious that he did not regret her turning down his offer to become his mistress. That knowledge, as much as she hated to admit even to herself, was a disappointment. Against her better judgement, she had secretly hoped that he was avoiding her because he did not want to lose control and ask her again.

Not that she wanted to be his mistress—because she did not. But it would be nice to know that he still found her desirable. She shook her head in bewilderment at her conflicting emotions. She had to stop this.

Sounds of commotion penetrated the salon door. Her heart jolted. The Countess must have arrived. Hastily wiping her hands on her skirts and wishing she had had time to clean up and change to a clean dress, she rushed into the hall and on to the foyer.

Boxes and trunks were strewn around with more coming in. The Countess stood in the middle of everything and presented her cheek for Ravensford to kiss, which he dutifully did.

Beside the Countess stood a young girl who looked barely out of the schoolroom. Her bright blonde hair was cut short and fashionably frizzed around her elfin face. Her blue eyes sparkled with curiosity, and her feet danced. She was as excited as a person could be and not explode.

Mary Margaret smiled. The child would be a delight.

The Countess caught sight of her. 'Miss O'Brien, I want you to meet my goddaughter, Miss Annabell Winston.'

Annabell turned her dazzling smile on Mary Margaret. 'I am so pleased to meet you, Miss O'Brien. Godmother has told me about everything you have been doing.'

'Don't gush so,' the Countess said.

The girl quieted, but nothing could dim her exuberance.

'Miss O'Brien has worked diligently and accomplished a great deal,' Ravensford said.

'I shall be inspecting everything once I have rested,' the Countess said, sweeping up the stairs. 'Is my room prepared?'

'Yes, my lady,' Jones, the butler said, following in the Countess's wake.

Mary Margaret followed more slowly, trailing the Earl and Annabell. She had overseen the final preparations, arranging the flowers and ensuring that the fire was properly laid.

The Countess entered her rooms in a swathe of servants and family and stopped. Her gaze swept the immaculate blue drapes and bedspread. She took in the rich carpet underfoot.

'Whoever brought those flowers in here should be let go, Andrew. You know I loathe lilacs.'

Mary Margaret paled and wanted to sink into the floor, but she could not let the Countess think someone else was responsible. If anyone suffered, it should be she.

'My lady, I am truly sorry. I did not know you disliked the flowers when I brought them in.'

The Countess turned on her. 'I should have known. Next time check before you do anything.'

'Yes, my lady.' Mary Margaret bowed her head in submission even though she railed at the Countess's high-handed treatment. This was nothing different from when she had been in Ireland.

'You are dismissed,' the Countess said, unfastening her cape and letting it fall to the rug where it was quickly picked up by her maid, Jane.

Mary Margaret breathed a sigh of relief and made her escape. Things did not look good for her stay in London. Thank goodness her quarterly salary was due soon. Somehow she would return to Ireland then and convince Emily to leave Thomas and come live with her. She would not let herself think anything else.

Ravensford waited for the door to close behind Mary Margaret before turning to his mother. 'That was unnecessary, Mother. She has worked harder than anyone to ensure the house is ready.'

The Countess eyed him narrowly. 'I will not be spoken to like that by you, Andrew.' She turned away from him. 'Annabell, you will be in the Green Room. Jones will see that your luggage is taken there.'

Always the perfect butler, Jones managed to keep his face blank, but his gaze darted to the Earl.

Ravensford spoke smoothly. 'That won't be possible, Mother. The Green Room is already occupied. The Rose Room has been prepared for Annabell.' He turned to the chit. 'The colour will compliment you more than the Green Room ever could.'

Annabell giggled. 'You always were a gallant, Ravensford. I see that you have not changed.'

He made her a playful bow. 'I aim to please.'

'Well, you don't please me, Andrew.' The Countess cut across their banter. 'Have whoever is in the Green Room removed.'

Ravensford gave his parent a noncommittal look. 'No, Mother. Everything is fine the way it is.'

'Out,' the Countess said, waving her hand at everyone. When she and Ravensford were alone, she said, 'You have put that woman in there, haven't you? Well, I won't have it. She is not a proper companion to start, and even if she were, the Green Room is for important guests.'

Ravensford sauntered to the window and watched the carriage traffic on the street below. 'I believe this conversation is taking us nowhere, Mother. Miss O'Brien is staying where she is, and Annabell will be perfectly happy in the Rose Room.' He turned back to his mother before moving to the door. 'I hope you will be well enough to come down for dinner. Gaston has prepared your favourite foods, and you know how temperamental he can be.'

'Andrew—'

He walked out. Leaving his mother in a snit was not the best of things to do, but he had no intention of obeying her orders. His only worry was that she would make Mary Margaret's life miserable. He knew his mother well.

Thank goodness his parent did not know he had asked Mary Margaret to be his mistress. Any hint of that and the Countess would throw Mary Margaret into the street without a second thought.

At least he had kept away from her. He had learned early in life that there was no sense in tempting himself with something he could not have. Time cured everything—or made everything available.

A week after the Countess and Annabell's arrival, Mary Margaret donned her best gown, which had been her second best before the accident with the sea. It was dove grey wool, much like her other two dresses. Instead of dancing slippers, she wore her everyday shoes, the worn black leather doing nothing to enhance her toilet.

She turned away from the full-length mirror. She had never had more than a hand-held mirror her entire life. This one, where she could see her entire self, was an unheard-of luxury. Although right now she could do without it.

Determined to make the best of an awful situation, she carefully braided her waist-length hair and piled it atop her head. The style was a departure for her, but she knew it showed her long neck to advantage. She carefully loosened a few strands near her temples so that they curled around her eyes. Next she pulled her gold locket from underneath her bodice so that it showed like a bright spark.

Her reflection in the mirror looked like what she was—a poor companion.

Pride straightened her shoulders. She would not fare well at this ball, but there was nothing she could do. The Countess was not going so she must chaperon Annabell. Things could be worse. Annabell could be like her godmother. Instead, the girl was young, lovely and sweet.

On that uplifting thought, Mary Margaret marched from the room resolved to get through the evening ahead. At least she was not Emily, at home in Ireland wondering when Thomas would drink too much again and lose his temper.

Yes, things could be much worse.

Ravensford put Annabell's white satin-lined velvet cape around the chit's shoulders. She had been early, eager to experience her first visit to Almack's.

Ravensford heard footsteps on the landing and

looked up to see Mary Margaret. She filled his senses.

''Tis a good thing my cape is securely fastened, Ravensford,' Annabell said with a touch of humour. 'Otherwise it would be on the floor from your lack of attention.'

Ravensford gave her a quick grin, but his focus returned to Mary Margaret. He watched her finish descending the stairs. She moved with the flowing grace of the cat she so reminded him of. His loins tightened.

The weeks of avoidance had done nothing to cool his ardour. Too bad she had refused his offer of *carte blanche*. Too bad she was a potential thief, he told himself, determined to stop reacting to her. It was bad enough that he desired her. Worse that he had so little control over his response to her. No other woman in his life had ever made him react as completely and physically as she did. It was an unsettling situation.

'Oh, Mary Margaret,' Annabell said, her youthful voice full of disappointment. 'Why did you not tell me you don't have a ball gown? I would have loaned you one of mine.'

'Silly child. Nothing of yours would fit me. I am just fine the way I am. A chaperon is not supposed to be fashionable, merely present.'

'But I don't want you to be a drab mouse.' Annabell's lips formed a pretty little pout.

'You are a good-hearted child,' Mary Margaret said. 'Now we must go. It might be fashionable to be late, but this is your first time. We must make sure that you have plenty of opportunity to savour the event.'

'You always think of me,' Annabell said.

Mary Margaret smiled.

Ravensford watched the byplay, free to study Mary Margaret without having her aware. Annabell was right. She looked like a drab little tabby. Anger at his mother tightened his jaw. His parent had thrown Mary Margaret into the clutches of the *ton* without a thought for the woman's wardrobe or feelings.

The thoughtlessness was typical.

To cover his unreasonable reaction, he said, 'Jones, fetch Miss O'Brien's cape. The weather will turn colder.'

Always the perfect butler, Jones turned to Mary Margaret for directions. She said calmly, too calmly, 'That will not be necessary.'

'Yes, it will.' Ravensford had had enough. He was taking charge and they were leaving. When she did not answer, he said, 'Well?'

She turned coldly to him. 'I do not have a cape.'

'Of course you do. You wore it on the trip here.'

She eyed him as though he was an exotic specimen. 'Yes, and the continual rain and mud ruined it. Now may we leave?'

He turned to Jones. 'Fetch one of the Countess's evening capes.'

The butler blanched. 'Yes, my lord.'

'Tell Jane that I order it.'

'Yes, my lord.' Looking like a man about to face his worst nightmare, Jones headed up the stairs.

'Oh, Godmother won't be happy,' Annabell said softly.

Irritation made Ravensford sharp. 'I don't care what she likes or doesn't like. Miss O'Brien requires a cape. Mother will provide.'

Annabell eyed him askance but kept any further opinions to herself. Mary Margaret turned away from him so that he could not tell how she felt. However, her shoulders were tensed and her hands clenched.

A fresh spurt of ire made him stalk away. 'I will be in the library. Notify me when the cape arrives and we can finally be on our way.'

He was being unreasonable and he knew it. His mother was always inconsiderate of others and particularly of servants and those she felt beneath her. She was the reason he had decided to champion those less fortunate than himself. He had watched his father, caught by love, flinch every time his wife slighted someone. Father had been a mild man, concerned about others. Ravensford had always thought it his father's misfortune to love a woman so completely different from him. But their marriage had been happy. They had been devoted to each other.

Now he had to contend with Mother. But he had learned young that loving someone did not necessarily mean you liked that person.

As he had expected, Jones sought him out. 'My lord, the Countess requests your presence.'

Ravensford tossed off the remainder of the whiskey he had just poured. 'Thank you, Jones.'

The butler bowed and withdrew.

Ravensford barely glanced at the two women as he passed them in the foyer. Standing up to his mother was something he rarely did. Normally he let her actions pass him by. Her being in Ireland most of the year made things much easier between them. He mounted the stairs, determination hardening his resolve to make his mother do yet another thing she would not like—and all for Mary Margaret O'Brien.

The Countess bade him enter after making him wait for several minutes outside her door. His mood was not improved.

She sat beside a dainty Chippendale table, her chair a match. A book lay open on her lap.

She turned a baleful eye on him. 'What is the meaning of this, Andrew? The chit is a servant. She has no need for one of my cloaks. Nor will I loan her one.'

Ravensford felt his teeth grinding, but he managed to keep his voice cool. 'Then give her one.'

'Andrew, you overstep yourself. Your father would never have treated me like this.'

'Nor would I if you would be generous enough to help Miss O'Brien out.'

'I pay her. Let her purchase her own clothing. And you have ensconced her in one of the best suites. That is more than sufficient.' She waved a delicate white hand as though to push the entire situation away.

Many times in his life he had been tempted to throttle his mother, but never so much as now. This anger was out of character. Another thing to lay at Mary Margaret O'Brien's feet.

Tired of arguing, he strode past her and into her dressing room. Riffling among her clothes, he grabbed the first cape he came to. Holding it in a clenched fist, he re-entered his mother's boudoir.

The Countess stood, her white hair a halo around her furious face. 'How dare you, Andrew. Put that back. Now.'

Ignoring her, he stalked to the door, opened it

and left. She was too conscious of appearances to follow him. Downstairs, he flung the black velvet cape around Mary Margaret's shoulders.

'We are leaving.'

Chapter Eight

Ravensford reached the front door before Jones, who rushed up and held it open. Outside, the carriage waited. A footman hurried to open the door and let down the steps, then handed Annabell and Mary Margaret inside. Ravensford followed, flinging himself down on the seat beside Annabell. He noted that Miss O'Brien had her back to the horses.

A sardonic smile curved his lips. 'I see that you know your place, Miss O'Brien.'

'As do you, my lord.'

Her sharp words were a slap in the face. He nodded ironically. 'I am out of line. Pardon me.'

'Whatever possessed you, Ravensford,' Annabell said. 'I could have loaned Mary Margaret a cape.'

'One I have no need of.'

Ravensford scowled from one to the other. 'Typical.'

He put a stop to discussion by rapping his cane against the ceiling, telling the coachman to go. The carriage lurched forward.

No one spoke for some time. As they turned down King Street where Almack's was situated, the excitement was too much for Annabell who began to chatter. Soon both women were caught up in anticipation. Ravensford, who had cut his eyeteeth on Almack's, expected an evening of boredom.

They entered to the general hubbub of dowagers sitting in chairs along the wall, couples performing a country dance, and clusters of men flirting with chits. Normal.

Ravensford scanned the room, looking for any familiar faces. He caught Mrs Drummond Burrell frowning at them. Her attention was on Mary Margaret. The Duke of Wellington had been denied admission because he was not in evening dress; Ravensford wondered if the patroness was about to come over and tell Mary Margaret she could not attend. It would be a fitting end to an awful beginning.

Just as Mrs Drummond Burrell took a step toward them, Sally Jersey caught her arm and whispered something. Both women glanced their way, Sally with a mischievous smile and Mrs Drummond Burrell with dislike. Ravensford took that to mean Sally had intervened.

He ushered his charges farther into the room and deposited them near a group of young bucks. He raised an eyebrow and one of the youths separated and came to them.

'Ravensford,' the young man said. 'Didn't expect you here. And with such lovely companions.'

Ravensford bit back a sharp retort. Potsford was always effusive where women were concerned. But the youth did not deserve the sharp edge of his tongue. It was not Potsford's fault this evening had started so abysmally and promised to continue on that way.

'Annabell, Miss O'Brien, may I present Mr Potsford. This is my mother's goddaughter, Annabell Winston, and her chaperon, Miss O'Brien.'

'Pleased to meet you.' Always on the lookout for an heiress, Potsford lost no time. Bowing to Annabell, he said, 'May I have the pleasure of the next country dance?'

She blushed delicately. 'Please.'

'Until then, may I escort you to the refreshment table?' he asked, offering his arm.

Blushing prettily again, Annabell laid her fingers on his arm. The two headed off.

'He will be disappointed,' Ravensford said drily.

'Why ever for?' Mary Margaret asked, defence of her charge making her raspy voice catch.

'Because she is not an heiress.'

'She is a delightful young woman and will make some lucky man a wonderful wife.'

'But not Potsford.'

'You members of the aristocracy are all alike.'

'Too often,' he drawled. 'Come dance with me.'

She scowled. 'You mock me, my lord. This is a waltz. Even I know a woman cannot dance the waltz unless a patroness has approved.'

'No,' he murmured, wondering why he did such outrageous things around her. 'I don't mock you. Or are you afraid?'

She angled her chin up. 'Afraid? Of what?'

He gave her a lazy smile. 'Of what I might do— or say.'

More than that, she was scared of what she might say or do. Much as she deplored her reaction to him, he made her blood pound and her stomach churn.

'No.' Even to her own ears, her voice sounded breathy and unsure.

He laughed outright. 'Stay here.'

Mary Margaret watched him angle through the crowd. His broad shoulders, clad in a bottle-green evening coat, were an arresting sight, as were his muscular thighs in black satin casing. To her mind, he was the most attractive man here. Seeing other women follow him with their gaze, she knew her opinion of him was widely held. He was probably going to find a woman of his own station to dance with.

She turned away, her chest tight. The last thing she wanted was to see him with another woman.

She found a single chair in a corner and sat down. She did not have to be in Annabell's pocket, only make sure the girl did not dance more than twice with any one man and stayed out of dark areas. At least she could enjoy the music. She had always loved to dance and sing. Music brought her solace.

She felt a tingling awareness seconds before she heard Ravensford's voice.

'I have someone I want you to meet,' he said.

Surprised that he had come back, Mary Margaret jumped up. The woman with him was the same one she had seen earlier talking to another woman and smiling at Ravensford. She must be his latest interest, although she appeared a little old for him.

'Lady Jersey,' he said, 'I would like you to meet Miss O'Brien. She is the chaperon of my mother's goddaughter. Miss O'Brien, this is Lady Jersey, one of the patronesses.'

The woman arched one immaculate brow. 'How do you do, Miss O'Brien? Now, I would like to present the Earl of Ravensford for your consideration as a waltz partner.'

This was the last thing she had expected. There was a spark of mischief in Lady Jersey's eyes and an intense emotion in Ravensford's that she could not identify. Both waited for her answer.

She took a deep breath and gave the Earl her hand. There was nothing else she could do without drawing attention to them.

'Thank you, Sally,' Ravensford murmured.

'My pleasure,' Lady Jersey said before bubbling laughter escaped her red lips. 'I shall dine out on this for many a day. The much sought-after Earl of Ravensford needing help to get a chit to dance with him. Oh, yes, I shall enjoy telling this one.'

Ravensford winced but said nothing more.

Mary Margaret heard what Lady Jersey said, but dismissed it as a woman teasing an attractive man. She wanted to run. The last thing she wanted was for this man to hold her as intimately as the waltz required. When he slipped his arm around her waist, the dance floor tilted. She needed all her willpower not to melt against him.

Instead, she demanded, 'What do you think you are doing? I am here as a chaperon, barely one level up from a servant. I cannot dance with you. What will people say? What will your mother say?'

He drew her close. 'No more than they already are.'

She gasped and looked around. People watched them, some annoyed, others amused and more scandalised. She stiffened.

'I don't belong here.'

'You have as much right as anyone.'

'I have never waltzed.' Desperation made her voice husky.

He grinned raffishly. 'Follow me. I won't lead you astray.'

He dipped her and twirled her, making her momentarily lose her train of thought. It was hard to concentrate when a man you were inexorably drawn to held you tightly and made the world around you spin.

'I am not of your world,' she managed breathlessly. 'They know it. Lady Jersey knew it when she introduced us.'

His grip intensified until less than the proper twelve inches separated them. His face was close enough that she could see the golden striations in his green eyes. His nostrils flared.

'"My world", as you put it, is hide-bound. Too many of us are only concerned with our own entertainment.'

She stared up at him, seeing a determination that

she had not realised he possessed. 'Are you a reformer?'

His mouth, those wonderful lips that she always fantasised on hers, twisted. 'I try.'

She had wondered. Too many times she had watched him reach out to those beneath him not to have pondered why he did so.

'Is that why you are so active in Parliament?'

'For the most part.'

The knowledge that he cared enough for those less fortunate than himself to stand up in Parliament and fight for their rights hit her with a jolt. Not only was he a handsome man with great wealth, but he was a caring man. The attraction she had felt for him from the beginning increased beyond anything she had thought possible.

The music swirled around them. She moved with him, their feet gliding over the floor. She felt removed from reality, caught in a dream with only him and her. He was her perfect lover.

Heaven help her. Heaven help her heart.

She swayed to a stop in his arms. The notes faded away. The other couples drifted from the floor.

He held her attention.

'Doing it too brown,' a male voice drawled.

Mary Margaret started. Behind Ravensford stood a man as dark of visage as her imagination often painted the devil. Silver wings flew from his temples and a scar ran the length of his right cheek. Dark eyes, nearly black, watched them dispassionately. His entire person was slightly dishevelled, almost disreputable, but she knew that could not be or he would not have been allowed inside. Almack's was much too proper to allow in a rogue.

'Ah, Perth,' Ravensford said without turning. 'Always in the nick of time.'

Perth shrugged. 'I do my best. But there are times when no one can help you.'

Ravensford gave a mirthless chuckle. 'Spoken like a true friend.'

He still had not released her, and Mary Margaret, realising they were creating a spectacle, tried to step away. Several young girls tittered behind their hands.

'But already too late,' Perth said, holding out his hand to Mary Margaret. 'May I introduce myself since Ravensford is remiss. I am Perth.'

'The Earl of Perth,' Ravensford added.

'Another earl,' Mary Margaret said, giving Perth her hand. He brushed her fingers with his lips.

'My pleasure. Would you care for some rataffia? Yes? Ravensford will be happy to get it.' There was a wicked gleam in his eye.

'Always in command.' Ravensford touched his brow in salute before moving away.

Mary Margaret was nonplussed. With Ravensford went her sense of warmth and security, although she would never tell him that and could barely admit it to herself. She did not have the experience to deal with a man of Perth's calibre. She slanted him a glance through lowered lashes. She had a feeling he could be as cruel as he could be kind, if he was ever kind. Yet he had put himself forward to interrupt the scene she and Ravensford had created.

He guided her to a seat. 'The old Countess hired you to play nursemaid to her goddaughter?'

She nodded, still not sure what to say to him.

'Don't pay Ravensford's mother any mind. She has been the trial of his life.'

She nodded again, knowing now that she should say nothing. The last thing a servant or employee should do was talk about her employer.

His mouth split into a grin showing white teeth. Much like a predator.

Mary Margaret cudgelled her brain for an excuse to get away. Jumping up, she said, 'I see Annabell over there with Mr Potsford. I should go to her.'

He made her an ironic bow. 'As you wish.'

She did not wait.

'You certainly scared her off,' Ravensford said. Having just arrived with the drink, he now sat on the vacated chair.

'Your inamorata is a scared tabby. I thought you more adventurous than this.' He gave Ravensford a lascivious grin. 'Especially after taking up with the "Delightful Delilah". Lord, but she led you a merry chase.'

'She did.' Ravensford smiled at remembered antics. 'I am getting too advanced in age to deal with another such as she. Too exhausting.'

'Hence the tabby?'

His friend's disparagement of Mary Margaret was oddly irritating. 'She is no tabby. And I have not taken up with her. She is my mother's companion and Annabell's chaperon.' He cast Perth a wicked glance. 'And she has already turned down my offer.'

'Aha. That explains everything. I've never seen you dance like that with one of your mother's companions,' Perth said drily.

Determined to shake Perth from his high perch, Ravensford stated, 'She plans to steal something from my parent. I am keeping a close eye on her to see that she is unsuccessful. I thought that having her for a mistress would keep her nearby.'

'Ah…everything is clear.'

He angled to face Perth, intending to set him straight when his attention was caught by Annabell. 'Blast that chit. She can't go off with Potsford.'

'Definitely not. The puppy is as broke as shattered crockery.'

Perth's sarcasm was lost on Ravensford as he headed off. The last thing he needed was for Annabell to add another indiscretion to this evening—and hers would be much worse. Mary Margaret was not on the Marriage Mart and neither was he. Annabell was.

He caught up with the pair just as Mary Margaret gripped Annabell's arm. 'I believe Mr Potsford has taken ill and must leave, Annabell. Let us not keep him.'

Potsford looked ready to protest until he saw Ravensford over Mary Margaret's shoulder.

The Earl took Annabell's elbow in a firm hold. 'Miss O'Brien is right. It is time we left as well.'

'Quite right. Getting late,' Potsford said, edging away.

'But…but I don't want to,' Annabell said.

Ravensford stared her down. 'But you are.'

'His lordship is right, Annabell,' Mary Margaret said. 'The Countess will be wondering where we are and curious about the night.'

'I doubt that,' Annabell said rebelliously. But after an admonishing look from Mary Margaret, she acquiesced. 'I shall stop at her room if she is still awake and tell her everything. She always talks about how exciting her first Season was, she will enjoy this.'

Mary Margaret gave the girl a warm smile. 'I thought you would.'

Ravensford doubted that his mother cared about anything except her own comfort, but perhaps he judged her too harshly. She had always listened to his tales of wonder and woe. It was just when people she considered beneath her were involved that his parent could be unlikable and uncaring.

While they waited for the carriage to come around, he watched the two women. With all their differences in station and character, they seemed to genuinely like each other.

Mary Margaret O'Brien was a conundrum. She was educated, gentle and caring, yet she intended to steal from his mother. While part of him couldn't blame her, he knew the plan had been concocted in cold blood, something he would have thought the woman laughing softly with Annabell was incapable of. But he knew differently. He could still hear her wonderful voice agreeing to the deed.

The carriage arrived and they returned home with the two women discussing the evening and him watching the companion. The candles from the coach lanterns cast first shadows, then light, on the sharp angles of Mary Margaret's face. One minute she was a tigress, all temptation and dark. The next she was a kitten playing gently with Annabell.

At all times she was a mystery.

Chapter Nine

Mary Margaret breathed deeply of the roses that surrounded the tiny white iron gazebo. Like the Gothic folly the Countess had in Ireland, this gazebo had become her sanctuary. No one ever found her here.

She had peace and quiet to think about last evening. She had had a wonderful time. Ravensford had made the waltz seem like a part of them. For a large man he was very graceful. Even though he had held her closer than proper, she had not minded. Being close to him was too thrilling for anything else to matter.

She sighed and closed her eyes, wanting to relive the experience again.

'Miss, his lordship requires your presence in the library.'

Mary Margaret sat bolt upright. She had not

heard anyone. Now a young girl stood in front of her twisting her hands.

'Susan, you startled me. I did not hear you.'

'Pardon, miss.'

Still the girl did not stop wringing her hands. 'Whatever is the matter, Susan?' Mary Margaret stood and went to the girl. She put a gentle hand on the servant's shoulder. 'Never say you are afraid of me?'

'Oh, no, niver.' The young girl sighed. 'Not you, miss. But, his lordship is in an awful hurry…'

Mary Margaret gave the maid a quizzical look. 'Then I will go upstairs and freshen up. Then I will report to him.'

'Yes, miss.'

Mary Margaret smiled at the girl who was barely more than a child. 'What are you afraid of? Surely not the Earl.'

Susan chewed her bottom lip. 'I shouldn't be talkin' to ye, miss. But…his lordship is changed since he returned from Ireland. All of us says so.'

Curiosity filled Mary Margaret. Susan was right in that Mary Margaret should not be gossiping with the servants, but then she was very nearly one herself.

'How?' she asked, hoping she only sounded mildly interested.

The girl sidled closer and her voice lowered.

'Temper, miss. He has a temper. Niver had one befores. Like he's bothered awful by somethin'.'

Mary Margaret's heart skipped a beat. It could not be because she had refused his offer to be his mistress. Nor could it be because of Thomas's plan to have her steal some of the Countess's jewellery. Ravensford knew nothing about that. Still…

'Oh.' Her voice scraped. In spite of her conviction that the Earl did not know, her nerves had still got the better of her. She started again. 'Oh? I thought he was always volatile.'

Although when she thought about it, he had not shown any impatience or anger during the discussion she had sat in on between him and his mother before they left Ireland. She would have lost patience with the Countess. The woman was as scatterbrained as she was high in the instep. Yet he was constantly losing his temper with her.

'No, niver, miss. He's ever so easy goin' and friendly. But no more.' Her shoulders drooped as though she had lost something personal.

Mary Margaret wondered at the girl's reaction. Ravensford had always seemed concerned about his people, but she had not realised how involved with him they were. He must be a good employer and landlord.

'And just now you were afraid that if I refused his summons he would be angry with you.'

'Yes, miss.'

'Don't worry, Susan. I will go. But first I must tidy up a bit.'

Mary Margaret left the girl in the kitchen and went up to her room. Alone, she went to the full-length mirror. Her hair needed straightening; pieces had come loose from the chignon and curled around her eyes like errant tendrils of thread.

Unbidden came the memory of Ravensford brushing her hair back from her face after she had nearly drowned. His warmth and concern had eased much of her panic. At the time, she had not recognised how his strength had sustained her. Realising now was like being struck by lightning—searing and surprising.

When had she come to depend on him so much? She did not know. It had just happened. She had only been in his company a month.

This was awful.

Right now, this instant, she could imagine his touch on her, his fingers warm and sure against her skin—as they had been last night. Never in her wildest flights of imagining had she envisioned the ecstasy of being caught up in his arms, dancing the waltz. Never.

Delight suffused her. Using the hairbrush as Ravensford's hand, she began to dance. She hummed the waltz tune from last night as she twirled around the room, smiling up at her imaginary partner. Faster and faster she went, her emotions soaring.

'Umph!'

It was a rude awakening to trip against a pile of books she had stacked in the middle of the room preparatory to returning them to the Earl's library. She sat down on the floor with a thump, the brush falling from her fingers. Her foot hurt like the dickens where she had smacked it.

She sighed. This loss of control was getting her nowhere. She had to rein in her imagination and her emotions.

A knock on the door reminded her that she had to attend Ravensford. Susan was very likely worried sick that she had changed her mind and was not going downstairs.

'I am coming,' she said loudly enough for the maid to hear.

She rose and dropped the brush that had started it all on to the dresser. A quick glance in the mirror showed her hair still looking unkempt and a sheen on her face that flushed her cheeks and reddened her lips. She was a sight.

But she was already late. She wet her hands in the ewer and quickly slicked them over her hair, hoping the strands would stay in place long enough for this meeting.

Mary Margaret straightened her shoulders and headed toward the library where she knocked and waited for Ravensford's permission to enter. Silly pictures of her waltzing around her room brought a smile to her lips, lips suddenly dry. And her palms were wet. No matter how she tried to prepare herself for his presence, her reaction to him always overwhelmed her better sense. It scared her.

His baritone 'Come in' jolted her into action. She stumbled through the door as soon as the footman opened it. He shut it behind her before she even realised she was in the library.

A slight smile curved Ravensford's lips. 'Do you always make an entrance like that? If so, you should be on the stage.'

She flushed, but quickly regained her composure. 'I was woolgathering, expecting to be kept waiting longer than you did, my lord.'

'Procrastination is not one of my failings,' he said, moving from behind the large mahogany desk where he had been sitting when she entered. He bore down on her. 'How many times have I told you to call me Ravensford? After all we have been through it is more appropriate.'

She felt like he was suffocating her with his nearness. She took a step back.

'I cannot do that.'

He moved closer, frowning. 'Don't give me any

of that nonsense about being a servant. You are no more a servant than I am a duke.'

She raised an eyebrow. 'Exactly, my lord. It would never have occurred to me to make the comparison you just did. That more than anything says I am a servant.'

A strange light entered his eyes. 'Did you feel like a servant last night? You didn't act like one. Not in my arms.'

His words caught her off guard. They were the last things she expected him to say. In her mind she was the one who still thought of last night. The dance should be gone from his memory by now.

Unconsciously she raised one hand in a symbolic attempt to fend him off. His stance dared her to lie. She took a deep breath, prepared to tell him anything but the truth.

'No,' she whispered, appalled at her answer even as the word slipped out.

He was beside her in a second, his hands gripping her shoulders. 'I knew it.'

Shivers chased down her spine, followed by heat that curled in her stomach. His mouth was inches from hers and coming closer. The breath caught in her throat. Her gaze clung to his. She did not want to miss anything.

'You are supposed to close your eyes,' he said, chuckling deep in his chest.

Lethargy crept through her limbs as she did his bidding. She could feel the warmth of his breath against her skin. This was how she remembered him.

His mouth closed over hers and her heart jumped. His lips teased at hers, his tongue trailing along her flesh. His hands roamed over her back until one settled at her waist and pulled her close, so close she could feel his chest rising and falling. She swayed into him, opening her mouth to allow him to deepen the kiss.

The hand at her waist slid lower until it cupped the swell of her hip. The other hand rose to the base of her neck and angled her head to one side so he penetrated better.

Her heart pounded. The blood rushed in her ears. Her stomach rioted. Never, in her entire life, had she felt like this. Alive and tingling, ready for anything.

He broke away from her, panting. She whimpered, her hands circling his neck as she tried to pull him back.

He laughed, but it was shaky. 'Easy, sweetheart. This is not the place, much as I want to finish what we have started.'

She blinked and came to her senses. Slowly. Slowly enough that his lips brushed hers before he finally released her.

She swayed and grabbed on to the nearest object, the back of a chair. He was close enough that she could see the black of his pupils. They seemed to fill his entire eye. He looked as though he had just woken, sensual and…and something she could not explain. Excited? Hungry?

She felt bereft, his warmth no longer enfolding her.

'I will come to your room tonight,' he murmured, bending just enough for his lips to brush hers.

His mouth on hers struck sparks that she feared would start an inferno inside her. She closed her eyes and tried to control her reaction to him. He was catnip and she was a cat. Her fingers shook from the effort not to reach out to him.

'After everyone has gone to bed,' he promised, his voice like a liquid caress along the curves of her body.

'After everyone has gone to bed,' she parroted. *After everyone has gone to bed.* Her eyes snapped open. She glared at him. 'No, you will not.'

A sardonic light entered his eyes, making them sharp as facetted emeralds. 'Coming to your senses?'

'How dare you? How dare you treat me like a…a lightskirt? I won't be your mistress, and every time you ask me you insult me. You treat me like

I am lower than the servant you continually say I am not.' She thrust her balled fists on her hips. 'Well, let me tell you. I would rather be the lowest of servants than your mistress.'

He stepped away, his eyes brooding, and made her a mocking bow. 'I hear you very well, Miss O'Brien. If you are not careful, the entire household will hear you.'

She sputtered to a stop as his words penetrated her indignation. She gulped air and turned away, unable to face him. She had behaved as wantonly as a loose woman. But she was not one.

When she had finally achieved a modicum of calm, she turned back to him. 'If you will excuse me, I have much to do.'

'I don't excuse you, Miss O'Brien.'

She froze in the act of moving to the door.

He stroked the signet ring on his left hand, drawing her attention to the fine sapphire. 'I want you to go to Annabell's modiste and get yourself a wardrobe suitable for a London Season.'

She gasped. 'You jest. First you try to seduce me, then ask me to be your mistress, and now you propose to send me to a modiste I cannot afford to patronise.'

'I am deadly serious, Miss O'Brien. And I intend to pay for everything.'

'You summoned me for this? Well, my answer is no. You will not pay for anything of mine.'

'Oh, but I will,' he drawled.

'No, you will not,' she reiterated. They were at it again. He was ordering her about and she was defying him.

'This continual contest of wills is boring, Miss O'Brien,' he said, turning away and going to sit behind his desk. 'Your appointment is at three. I shall expect you down here at half past two.'

Affronted to the core, she glared at him. 'I don't need anything. While I don't have much, and none of it is up to the standards of the *ton*, it is sufficient for me.'

'But not for me,' he stated.

She bristled. 'What have you to do with my wardrobe, pray tell?'

'It offends me.'

'Offends you!' Hurt, followed rapidly by anger, suffused her. 'How shallow.'

'I can be.' He shuffled a stack of papers and lined them up perfectly. 'I have sent word to Madame Bertrice that she is to provide you with a complete wardrobe.'

'You are mistaken, my lord.' She tipped her nose in the air.

'I think not.'

She ground her teeth together. They were very

close to a shouting match. Children would behave as they were. A smile tugged at her lips.

His eyes held a hint of humour. 'We are behaving as children.'

Some of the tension eased from her. Her shoulders relaxed. 'My exact thought.'

'Good. Then you will stop arguing with me and be at Madame's by three o'clock.'

Her face turned to stone. He was stubborn and used to having his own way. 'I did not say that.'

'I will have the carriage brought around by half past two.'

Mary Margaret knew a dismissal when she heard it. Just as well. She was done arguing with his lordship. She simply would not go. With barely a curtsy, she left, her ire up and her determination firmly in place.

Ravensford watched her go and knew she would disobey him—it was written in every line of her magnificent body. For the life of him, he did not understand why she brought out the stubborn streak he had worked so hard at eradicating. His father had told him once that the trait would cause him problems.

Shaking his head, he returned to his desk and re-read for the third time the Bill he intended to introduce to the Lords. His mind refused to concentrate.

Pictures of Mary Margaret O'Brien insisted on penetrating his thoughts. Her voice intruded on his dreams. She was an enigma he longed to unravel.

And that kiss. He had not intended for that to happen. After she had refused his offer of *carte blanche*, he had decided not to ask again. But kissing her had ignited a fire in him that nothing short of full possession could quench. He wanted her, and having sampled the excitement of her, he meant to have her. To hell with her plan to rob his mother.

As his mistress she would have enough jewels that she could give hers to the man who wanted her to steal his mother's. She would even have some left over. He would shower her with everything.

Now he had only to convince her that accepting his offer would be better than stealing.

That decided, he once again tried to read his Bill—and could not. As satisfying as the thought of having her for his mistress was, there was something wrong about it. He felt as though something was tarnished.

His secretary chose that moment to enter and Ravensford forced his attention to matters having nothing to do with his mother's companion.

Mary Margaret paced the confines of her room. The carriage waited for her. It would wait forever.

Part of her, the weak part, longed to have beautiful clothing. She had never had anything that was not serviceable. Some had been attractive in a practical manner, but never designed solely to make her look good.

But she was not allowing the Earl to buy her clothes. Men of his station bought clothes and other things for their mistresses. She was not his mistress. Nor was she going to be.

The hurt that had exploded in the library was now a dull ache. With time, she would make that go away too. So what if he desired her and nothing else? She had not even dreamed that he would desire her. She was a farmer's daughter with nothing to recommend her, not even stunning looks.

She stopped and her reflection in the mirror confronted her. The grey frock made her look drab, as though she was sick. In a fit of pique, she stalked to the mirror and, using all her strength, turned it to the wall.

'There,' she muttered, dusting her hands off. 'I shan't have to look at myself any more.'

The initial satisfaction was quickly replaced by the subdued knowledge that she knew by heart what the mirror showed. She did not need to see her reflection to know her clothing did nothing for her. And how she wished it might.

That weak part of her wanted to look pretty for

Ravensford. She did not want to be his mother's lowly companion who was good enough to steal a kiss from in the library when no one was around. She wanted to be the woman on his arm whom he proudly squired about town.

She wanted the moon. She was a fool. She dashed her fist across her eyes. She was not a watering pot.

A timid knock on the door, followed by Susan's hesitant, 'Miss, his lordship wants to know why you are late,' pulled Mary Margaret from her melancholy admission.

Surprise tightened her shoulders. She had not really expected Ravensford to keep track of the time and the appointment. She had thought he would be out about his business at the House of Lords, fully expecting her to do as he ordered. In her limited experience, men did not interest themselves in women's dress. Her father had never cared and nor did Thomas, whose money went on his own back.

Ravensford's persistence must come of the stubbornness she had glimpsed in him this morning. Nothing else that she could think of would explain this determination.

She crossed to the door, opened it and looked down at the maid's large brown eyes. She regretted putting the girl in the middle, but she was not going.

'Susan, please tell his lordship that I am indisposed and sorry for any inconvenience I might cause.'

The girl gulped. 'Yes, miss.'

'Oh, and would you please return this to the Countess?' Mary Margaret picked up the neatly folded black velvet cape and handed it to Susan.

After Susan took the garment, Mary Margaret closed the door behind the maid's retreating figure and crossed to the window. She looked out on the gardens, which were in full, riotous bloom. If she opened the glass, the scent of roses would fill the air. She did so and drew in a deep breath of the glorious smell. Perhaps she would be allowed to pick some of the blossoms and put them in a vase in her room. Then, perhaps not. It did not matter. She was mentally chattering, trying to keep herself from thinking of Ravensford's reaction when she did not appear as he commanded.

A second knock on the door froze her rambling mind.

'Who is it?' she rasped through stiff lips.

'Who do you think?' Ravensford asked, irritation evident in his inflection. 'I am not used to having my orders ignored.'

She closed her eyes and took a deep breath. 'I

told you before. I don't need those clothes. Nor will I go to the modiste.'

Her voice was raised enough to penetrate the thick wood of the door. She belatedly wondered how many servants were listening to this clash of wills. Why was he doing this?

The door opened. He stood, elbows akimbo, and glared at her. 'You are not missing the appointment.'

She crossed her arms over her chest. 'Yes, I am.'

His eyes narrowed. 'Do you want to embarrass Annabell again?'

'Embarrassment will not adversely affect her.'

He relaxed against the door jamb. 'But your clothing might. How you are dressed impacts on how the *ton* perceives Annabell. If you look poor and provincial, then she looks the same.'

Doubt sneaked through Mary Margaret's determination. 'That is silly.'

He shrugged. 'Of course, but that does not change it.'

The last thing she wanted was to hurt Annabell's chances of a successful Season. The girl was so excited and had such high expectations.

'What about Potsford last night? He did not seem the least bit put off that Annabell was with me.'

'I introduced them. He thought she was an heiress and he is on the lookout for one. He would not have cared if she had the face of a horse and the body of a hippopotamus.'

Mary Margaret flinched at the blunt, uncomplimentary description. 'What an awful picture that creates.'

'It was meant to,' he drawled. 'Appearances are everything to society. Annabell has a moderate dowry. She needs to marry well or at least respectably.'

She sighed. She had come to care for the girl, and the last thing she wanted to do was adversely impact on Annabell's Season.

'I will go, but only if the dresses I purchase are paid for from my salary.'

He straightened. For an instant, she thought mirth flashed across his face. She must have been mistaken because, when she squinted to see better, he was solemn. There was a twitch at his mouth but nothing more.

'Hurry. The horses have been kept waiting for far too long.'

He turned and left without a backward glance, as though he expected her compliance. His arrogance raised her hackles, but she had said she would go. Very likely he was returning to whatever business her failure to show had taken him from.

As dignified as a rushing woman could be, she

sped down the stairs and past the butler who held open the front door. She barrelled through the coach door the footman held and nearly into Ravensford. He grinned sardonically.

'Haste can make for some interesting seat mates.'

For what seemed like the hundredth time since she'd met him, she blushed. He constantly disconcerted her, although this last had been her own doing.

She plopped down. 'I did not think you were going. I am capable of doing this on my own.'

'But, I'm sure, not to my satisfaction.'

She drew herself straight, a set-down on the tip of her tongue, one she could not deliver. 'I am sure that nothing I can afford to buy will be to your satisfaction, my lord.'

She turned away as they set off. When he said nothing further, she tried to lose herself in the changing scenery. London was fascinating. She had never been outside of Cashel, and that country town was not even the size of one of London's hamlets.

But it was impossible to ignore him. She was too conscious of everything that had happened to them.

It was with relief that she felt the carriage slow down and stop. A small, very discreet door sat back from the street. There was no name on the outside. Nothing that she could see to tell the customer this was a dressmaker's shop, if it was. She gave Ravensford a questioning look.

'Madame Bertrice's. She does not advertise. She does not have to.'

He got out as soon as the footman opened the door and let down the steps. Turning back, Ravensford offered his hand.

Mary Margaret eyed his fingers warily. Even covered by fashionable gloves, they looked strong and demanding. She had no doubt that his touch would sear her flesh even though she also wore gloves. After their bout of lovemaking in the library, she did not trust herself near him. He did things to her.

But she could not ignore him. It was not done.

Taking a deep breath, she put her hand into his. She was right. Heat surged up her arm and tightened her chest. She cast one disconcerted glance at him before studiously watching where she put her feet.

'I won't let you fall, Miss O'Brien,' his honey-smooth baritone mocked.

'I never thought you would,' she answered primly, refusing to look him in the face and meet his unspoken challenge.

She had spent her life trying her best to meet

difficult situations without flinching, but now more than ever she felt cowardly. She had stood up to him as much as she thought herself capable of doing for one day.

The rest of the day, she was going to concentrate on not letting her desire for beautiful clothing overcome her determination to save for Emily. Soon she would be able to collect her quarterly wage. She would send it to Emily and tell her to leave Thomas. She could not get carried away here.

Chapter Ten

Once she was safely on the ground, his hand slid to her elbow and guided her toward the door. He opened it without knocking, and they entered one of the most elegant rooms Mary Margaret had ever been in.

Discreet beiges and creams, with just a hint of gold, covered the chairs, settees, floor and single window. Several delicate tables held vases with a few select flowers. A light floral scent filled the air.

Mary Margaret was entranced.

A petite woman glided toward them. She wore an elegant black gown with a single row of white lace at the bodice and wrists. Her blonde, almost white, hair feathered around a face smooth as a newborn's, yet her eyes spoke of years of experience.

'My lord Count,' she murmured, calling him by his continental title and offering her hand.

Ravensford took her fingers with grace and charm. Lifting them to his lips for the briefest of touches, he murmured, 'Madame Bertrice, allow me to introduce Miss O'Brien. She is the woman I spoke to you about.'

The modiste smiled at him before turning her attention to Mary Margaret. Bright blue eyes took in everything about Mary Margaret in what seemed seconds.

'Ah, just as you said, my lord,' the woman murmured, her accent settling into a brisk mode. 'I have just the thing. It was returned by one of my clients because the colour is too strong. It will be perfection on Miss O'Brien.' She crooked a finger at Mary Margaret. 'Come this way, please. We must see what alterations the gown needs. The original owner was not as shapely as you.'

Mary Margaret missed her step. She was not used to people speaking so openly of one's proportions.

Madame winked. 'You will find, Miss O'Brien, that the aristocracy is not so delicate as others in their mode of speech.'

Mary Margaret could only nod.

She was further discommoded to have to undress in front of Madame and an assistant. Both women behaved as though nothing was out of the ordinary, which gradually eased Mary Margaret's discomfort. She knew women who had their dresses made by others always disrobed thus, but she had never had that luxury.

The gown they brought out was stunning. The colour was the deep pink of wild roses, so rich it was nearly mauve. There was no adornment. They slipped the silken folds over her head and smoothed the material down her sides. The bosom had been let out and they quickly set about sizing it. Minutes later, they finished and turned her toward the single mirror.

Surely that was someone else, she thought, even though she knew intellectually that the reflection was hers. The deep pink put colour into her normally pale cheeks, even her lips. And the cut of the dress was masterful. She understood why Madame Bertrice did not advertise her location. Any woman seeing another in a dress like this would do anything to find out who had made it.

She looked like a long-stemmed rose, ready to sway in a passing breeze. She looked regal and beautiful. She knew, with a sinking heart, that she could never afford this dress on her salary, not even if she worked all her life.

She squeezed her eyes shut on her reflection.

Temptation was something she so rarely felt—until recently. First Ravensford and now this vanity.

'It is beautiful beyond words, madame,' she said regretfully. 'But I cannot afford this dress. I am truly sorry.'

The assistant tittered, only to be swatted sharply by Madame. Mary Margaret ignored the young girl the best she could, but it was not easy. Pride was a commodity she could not afford.

'Nonsense, mademoiselle. This gown is nothing. A *bagatelle*. To me, it is worthless.' She shrugged eloquently. 'I would be much better served by having someone of your uniqueness to wear it before the *ton*.'

Hope lit Mary Margaret's face. If only…

'Come, Miss O'Brien,' the modiste pursued, 'why would I tell you something that was not true, for I can see that you doubt me?'

'I don't disbelieve you, I simply cannot see how that can be. Any woman would be delighted to have this gown.'

'Then it is settled,' Madame stated.

'But I did not say I wanted to purchase—'

'Oh, but you did. Not in so many words, but I can see the longing you feel. Do not worry. The Count has provided me with much business in the past. The matter of this single garment is nothing.

Now come along and show his lordship what miracles a fine garment can create.'

Before Mary Margaret could protest further, Madame swept from the dressing room. The maid tittered again, watching her from lowered lashes. Mary Margaret felt trapped with nowhere to go but out to Ravensford. So be it.

Head high, shoulders back, she retraced her steps to Madame's receiving room. Ravensford was in conversation with the modiste and did not look up immediately. Mary Margaret took several deep breaths, wondering if she should return to the dressing room before either of them realised she was here. Just as she decided to do so, Ravensford glanced up. An arrested look came over him. Mary Margaret flushed to the top of the gown's bodice.

Ravensford had always found her to be an exotic beauty, but now she was devastating. The thin silk accentuated her full bosom and small waist. The colour made her eyes sparkle. His loins tightened painfully.

'Superb, madame,' he said softly, never taking his gaze from Mary Margaret. 'We will definitely take that one.'

'But of course,' Madame said complacently.

'I am glad you approve,' Mary Margaret said with a tinge of sarcasm, her deep husky voice rasping. 'Now, if you are both done studying me, I will go change.'

'By all means,' Ravensford said. As soon as she was out of the room he turned to Madame. 'I want a complete wardrobe for Miss O'Brien. Expense is not a consideration.'

'But of course.'

He eyed her sharply. 'Miss O'Brien is a lady of Quality.'

'I never thought otherwise, my lord.'

'Send this gown immediately along with a cape.'

'Tomorrow, my lord.'

Mary Margaret joined them and Ravensford contented himself with the knowledge that Madame would be discreet and her clothing impeccable. He escorted Mary Margaret to the waiting coach and could not resist the temptation to rest his hand on the small of her back as she entered the vehicle. He felt her skin jump under his fingers. She was not indifferent to him. Satisfaction curved his lips.

He followed her into the closed carriage. He had chosen this vehicle in the hope that fewer people would see them. Much as he wanted her to be dressed as befitted her beauty, he did not want everyone to know that he clothed her. He had no real excuse for doing so and others would realise that. The rumour mill would soon have them an *on-dit*, and while he intended to bed her, he did not intend for the whole world to know it. He had to trust to Madame's desire for more business from him and the loyalty of his servants that no one would talk.

He settled across from her, breathing deeply of her light lavender scent. He had always thought of the flower as a way to preserve and freshen clothing and linens. But from the moment he had first heard her speaking in his mother's library, the scent had taken on a sensual connotation that he knew would stay with him for life.

'You will wear the gown at the ball in Annabell's honour.'

She looked at him from the corner of her eye. 'I will wear it when and where I choose.'

He crossed one Hessian-covered leg over the other. 'You are the most argumentative woman it has ever been my misfortune to encounter. Can't you ever do as you are told without first fighting?'

She turned away and in a tight voice said, 'I have done as others have bid me all my life. But only you have tried to make me do things that I find to be inappropriate.'

Even as she finished speaking, a furtive look crossed her face. He grinned sardonically. She must be remembering the man who had ordered her to steal his mother's jewels.

'Are you sure?' he pursued.

Her chest rose and fell and she seemed to be struggling with a strong emotion. For a moment he was contrite, but he pushed the weakness away. Now was the time for her to tell him everything. Or at least hint at it.

'Yes,' she said shortly, refusing to meet his eyes.

His jaw hardened. There was more than one way to make a cat howl.

The remainder of the journey home passed in a strained silence that Ravensford did nothing to break. Let her stew in her own lies.

Ravensford fingered the grey pearl necklace. Matching ear drops, bracelets and a ring nestled in the nearby satin-lined box. The set would go perfectly with the mauve gown Madame Bertrice was altering. Unfortunately it had not arrived for tonight's visit to the Drury Lane Theatre. It did not matter. He could no more give Miss O'Brien the set to wear than he could fly to the moon. No matter that a large part of him wanted to defy convention and his mother in order to see how the Irish woman would look dressed as befitted her exotic beauty.

He returned the jewels to their case and handed them over to Stevens, who looked scandalised. Ravensford quirked one eyebrow.

The valet sniffed. 'Please allow me to get a fresh cravat, my lord. The one you are wearing has developed a crease where there should be none.'

Ravensford barely managed not to laugh out loud, which would have offended the valet. He should have known that Stevens cared nothing for the jewellery and everything for his master's toilet.

'Thank you, Stevens, but that won't be necessary. I realise that I am a trial to you but, as you know, I am not a dandy. I would not be happy to have you leave me for another, but I would understand.'

The valet gave his gentleman an aggrieved look. 'I could not leave. I waited years for you to hire me. You have the best shoulders and legs in all of London. You are a credit to my skills.' He sighed dramatically. 'If only I could impress upon you the importance of dress.'

Surprise stopped Ravensford from speaking for a moment. He had had no idea his valet felt so strongly about dressing him. For his part, he considered himself to be a well set-up man, but he had several friends he would describe as better physical specimens than himself. Perth was one.

Humbly, he said, 'Thank you, Stevens, for your devotion.'

The gentleman's gentleman gave his master a tight smile before handing over Ravensford's gloves and cane. Ravensford took the accessories and left. The ladies would be in the foyer shortly.

Half an hour later, Ravensford tapped his cane impatiently against his right leg and wondered why he had ever thought he should be on time. Women certainly did not consider promptness to be important.

He handed his *chapeau* to the butler. 'If the ladies come down, I will be in the library.'

He turned to leave and caught a glimpse of grey. Mary Margaret, dressed in her drab gown, and Annabell, dressed in white muslin trimmed with blue ribbons, were descending the stairs. His attention stayed on Mary Margaret. Even dressed dowdily, she aroused him.

She stood proudly, watching him. Her movements were delicate and flowing, her eyes brilliant as diamanté and her hair silky as a raven's wing. Dressed by Madame Bertrice, she would take the *ton* by storm.

She had stunned him in that pink dress. The neck had been lower than anything she ever wore, drawing his imagination to the hollow between her breasts. In many ways, it had been more erotic than her soaked chemise and pantaloons. The dress had been provocative.

He swallowed hard.

'Ravensford,' Annabell said in her high, light voice, 'you are being rude. You are putting Mary Margaret to the blush.' Her laugh filled the air.

He had to physically shake himself. His perusal had been too intense and too long. To hell with convention.

'I knew the gown would become you,' he said.

She looked nonplussed. 'This gown?'

Annabell's laughter trilled out.

Ravensford coughed to hide his own discomfiture. His mental picture of her in the pink dress had made him forget that she wore the grey. Never in all his thirty-two years had he behaved this gauche. In the end it was worth it. Her nervous laugh, low and throaty like a warm purr, filled the foyer and sent liquid desire coursing through his limbs.

'Thank you, my lord.'

'Andrew, what are we waiting for?' his mother said shrilly from where she stood on the landing, twenty feet above them. 'We will be late.'

He pulled his focus from Mary Margaret and made his parent an ironic bow. 'So we will, Mother. The coach is waiting.'

The butler showed the younger women out while Ravensford waited to assist his mother. The urge to throw convention to the wind and take Mary Margaret's arm was great, but he knew that doing so would only make matters worse for her. His parent would never condone his interest in the companion. He wondered why it mattered.

Mary Margaret kept her gaze focussed out the window of the carriage. The Countess and Annabell sat across from her, facing the driver. Ravensford sat beside her, his thigh brushing hers every time the coach lurched. She felt like a cat treading across Cook's oven, scorched and wary.

The scent of him filled her senses. He was so close that, if she turned her head, her mouth would brush his shoulder.

Memory of his kiss held her motionless. Her stomach rolled over slowly and her hands trembled. The urge to touch him, to invite his touch in return, filled her. Shivers chased sparks down her spine.

She closed her eyes and forced herself to remember why she was here, and it was not to be seduced by the Earl of Ravensford. In days her first quarter would be complete. Once her wages were in her hand, she could leave the Countess, somehow return to Ireland, and take Emily and Annie away from Thomas. That was why she was here.

She sighed with relief when the carriage finally stopped. The Countess and Annabell descended first. Ravensford followed, turned back to her and offered his hand. She stared at his gloved fingers, telling herself that allowing him to help her down would not make her breath go short and her stomach clench. She lied to herself and knew it.

Fighting to keep from trembling, she put her hand in his. His fingers closed over hers. Her eyes met his, their gazes locked. Her world narrowed to him and his touch. Nothing mattered, not her sister Emily, not her niece Annie, not the people around them.

No matter how many times he helped her from a carriage—and it seemed he did so constantly— she did not think she would ever become inured to his touch. For her, he was magical.

'Andrew,' the Countess demanded, rapping their clasped fingers with her closed fan.

He glanced at his mother and the spell broke. Mary Margaret jerked her arm back and hid her hand in the folds of her skirt.

'Mary Margaret,' the Countess said imperiously, 'see to Annabell, as you should have been doing all the time.'

Mary Margaret nodded, resisting the urge to dip a curtsy. Afraid to look at Ravensford and see his disgust at her weakness in succumbing to him yet again, she skirted away, holding her head proudly as her mother had taught her. The Countess might treat her as a nonentity, but she did not have to act downtrodden.

Annabell frowned at the situation. 'Godmother can be the most autocratic person in the world. Pay no mind to her, Mary Margaret.'

The younger girl linked her arm through Mary Margaret's and steered them to the doors where they waited for the other two. Mary Margaret could just hear the Countess's hissed words.

'Andrew, have you no pride? The chit is a servant, and barely that. Bed her if you must, but don't ogle her in public.'

Mary Margaret blanched and glanced at Annabell to see if the girl had heard. Annabell was smiling at a young man who stood nearby, her attention fully occupied. Thank goodness.

Mary Margaret could not hear Ravensford's reply but imagined it was one of indignant denial.

The Countess swept past them, Ravensford at her side. Mary Margaret and Annabell hurried to keep up. They made their way to Ravensford's reserved box and took their seats, Annabell, the Countess and Ravensford in the front. Mary Margaret sat in the back, positioned to see over the shoulders of the other two women.

The first play of the evening was nearly over. A Shakespearean tragedy that she watched with such absorption it was a shock when someone entered the box and moved in front of her.

The young man from outside had come to chat.

Ravensford rose and offered his chair, which the visitor accepted with alacrity.

'Would you care for refreshment?' Ravensford asked, startling Mary Margaret further.

'No, thank you,' she murmured, glad her voice sounded calm and uninterested.

'Always composed and in control,' he murmured.

She blinked and said nothing, no riposte coming to her rescue. He gave her a searching study, his face showing nothing.

'Andrew!'

The Countess's shrill voice broke whatever had caught Ravensford's attention. Mary Margaret was not sure whether to be happy or regretful. As uncomfortable as his interest was, she also found that she enjoyed it. In all, it was a very disturbing conundrum.

The Earl made an elaborate bow in the general direction of his parent and sauntered off. Mary Margaret felt the Countess's angry gaze on her and studiously avoided looking at the woman. It would do no good. The Countess would still make her life miserable.

A flash of gold caught her eye. She looked in the direction of the gallery, squinting to better see over the distance. Bucks and dandies milled about the area just in front of the stage, many calling to the actresses.

There was the golden glint again. She leaned forward in her seat. A tall, slim man lounged against the far corner. He was impeccably dressed in evening clothes tailored to his frame. His attention was on her.

No. It could not be. He would never come all this way. Never. But...

He waved in her direction. Thomas.

Mary Margaret blanched. He had followed her here. Where were Emily and Annie? Had he left them in Ireland?

'I took the liberty of getting you some punch,' Ravensford said, his baritone seeming to come from just behind her right ear.

Her pulse jumped. She glanced back at him, hoping her countenance did not betray her unease. Had he seen her looking at Thomas? Had he seen Thomas looking at her? Surely if he had he would think it nothing but two people exchanging interested glances. He did not know Thomas.

But the Countess did.

Mary Margaret shivered.

'Here,' Ravensford murmured, setting the punch down. 'Where is your cape?'

She stared at him. His words meant nothing.

'Where is your cape?' he repeated.

She shook her head. 'I don't have one.'

'Yes, you do. I gave you my mother's,' he said patiently as though talking to a child.

She shook her head again. 'I gave it back.'

What was Thomas doing here? Was he going to contact her? Was he going to tell her to steal the jewels now? She shut her eyes.

Ravensford's hand on her shoulder brought her back to the present situation. 'That cape was yours. When I give you something, I expect you to keep it.'

She stared blindly up at him. He was making such a fuss over something so trivial. 'It was not yours to give. You cannot take something from someone else and say it is yours to give where you wish.'

His fingers tightened on her shoulder. 'Is that a philosophy you live by? Or is it just for me and that blasted cape?'

She blinked and her mouth worked, but nothing came out. He spoke almost as though he knew, but he could not. No one knew, not even Emily.

'It is a philosophy I believe in.'

Instead of replying, he moved on to his mother and Annabell. She sagged. Surreptitiously she looked back where Thomas had been. He was gone.

She chewed her bottom lip. Perhaps she had

been mistaken. The lighting was not that good. It was ridiculous to think Thomas would come this far. In his mind as long as he had Emily and Annie that was more than enough to get her to do his bidding. That was it. She had been mistaken. A guilty conscience had tricked her.

She heard shuffling and noticed that the man who had occupied the Earl's seat the entire time had stood and was giving Ravensford back the chair.

'No need, Higgins,' Ravensford said. 'I am capable of standing.'

'Know you are, Ravensford, but must be moving on. Miss Annabell says I may pay m'respects tomorrow.' He bowed his way out without ever glancing in Mary Margaret's direction.

Instead of watching the young man leave, she concentrated on the activity starting on the stage. The Countess might treat her as though she did not matter, but being completely ignored was worse. She felt as though she did not exist. It was an awful sensation.

'Don't mind Higgins,' Ravensford drawled. 'He's never been known for his good manners.'

Against her better judgement, she gave the Earl a grateful smile. He always seemed to know how she felt. For a second warmth and security enveloped her, but only for a moment. Having her employer's son empathise with her was not a good thing. Especially when she had conspired with someone to rob that son's mother.

The rest of the evening passed agonisingly slowly for Mary Margaret.

Ravensford searched the gallery for the blond man who had waved at Mary Margaret. If he had not seen her blanch and look like she had been landed a facer, he would have thought the man a would-be swain. Instead he wondered if there was some connection to the man in Ireland who had been ordering her about. Far fetched, he knew, but someone had to be available for her to pass the stolen goods to.

He would have to keep an even closer eye on her. The knowledge did not make him feel better. Even knowing he was making a mistake, he had allowed himself to get involved with the woman. He had even imagined getting to know her very well.

He had been weak, something he would be careful not to be again.

Chapter Eleven

Several days later, Mary Margaret sat in the garden behind the house while the Countess and Annabell napped. She took advantage of the quiet time to read Jane Austen's *Pride and Prejudice*. A tidy smile twisted her mouth as she lived through Mr Darcy's internal war with himself. He was high in the instep and it nearly cost him the woman he loved. She set the finished book down and stared into space. Miss Austen's book was the perfect romance of two people from different levels of society.

She had heard that even the Prince of Wales read Miss Austen's books. Knowing that made her feel less guilty that the story had taken her out of her own problems.

Every day she woke, dreading the possibility that Thomas might call or contact her. So far, he had not. That strengthened her belief that she had been mistaken that evening at Drury Lane. The Thomas she knew would have forced her to meet with him by now. Even knowing that, she still worried.

'Miss, you are needed in the foyer.'

She jerked. She had been caught in her thoughts and not heard the footman. She pushed her fear of Thomas away and made herself smile.

'Goodness, Jeremy, you startled me.' She grabbed the book and rose.

'Pardon, miss.'

She smiled at him. His face radiated anticipation, making her wonder why he had come to fetch her.

'Why am I required in the foyer?'

He grinned, showing crooked front teeth. 'A surprise, miss.'

'Hmm.'

Minutes later, she stood in shock. Footmen carried large boxes through the front door while others carried more large boxes up the stairs. A veritable treasure trove was passing by her, all headed for her room.

'What is all this?' she gasped.

'What is the meaning of this outrage?' the Countess demanded at the same time, her voice rising above the bustle. The older woman stood at the top of the stairs, her robe caught at her throat with white knuckled hands. Her eyes blazed.

All movement ceased.

'Miss O'Brien's wardrobe has arrived,' Ravensford drawled, breaking the frozen silence.

He had come into the house unnoticed while everyone apprehensively watched his mother. With nonchalance, he handed his hat, gloves and cane to the butler before moving to the farthest wall.

He appeared to find nothing out of the ordinary. Mary Margaret knew he understood perfectly well what was going on. His bland look of interest did not fool her. Drat the man.

Both Mary Margaret and the Countess glared at him. He returned their angry looks with disregard, as though what he had done were not totally unacceptable.

'Andrew, come to my rooms immediately.' The Countess's gaze swept the assembled servants and came to rest on Mary Margaret. 'The rest of you clear this nonsense from the house. I won't have it. Return it to wherever it came from.'

Mary Margaret wanted to sink into the floor. She wanted to go up in a puff of smoke and regain consciousness in Ireland. She wished she had never succumbed to Thomas's threats and taken employment with the Countess. If only she had been stronger, but Emily had been at stake.

In spite of all that, she held her head high and met the Countess's furious look. 'I quite agree with you, my lady. None of this should be here.'

Ravensford pushed away from the wall and sauntered toward her. Mary Margaret stepped around a footman whose hands were full of boxes.

'This is my house, ladies,' he said gently, almost too gently. 'And I decide what goes on here. I also decide how members of my household will dress and present themselves to the world.' He looked at one and then the other. 'Do I make myself clear?'

Mary Margaret felt her mouth drop and quickly snapped it shut. She dared not look at the Countess. Everyone said the Earl rarely defied his mother, yet he was doing so now. Someone would pay for this and it would very likely be her.

The Countess said nothing more, turning on her heel and stalking off. There was a noticeable easing of tension.

'Continue what you were doing,' Ravensford stated. 'Miss O'Brien, come with me.'

Her hackles rose. 'I—' She stopped herself.

Everyone's attention had shifted to her. The last thing she wanted to do was make the situation worse, if that were possible, by defying Ravensford. With a supreme effort, she relaxed her rigid shoulders and followed behind him as he led the way to the library. She could feel the stares of all the servants. Her shoulders itched from tension.

Ravensford held the door for her, having gestured the butler away. She walked past him, head high, eyes focussed straight ahead. She kept moving until she had put the distance of the room between herself and the Earl's desk before stopping and turning back to face him. Somehow it did not feel far enough away.

'Feel safe?' He moved to his desk and poured a glass of the amber-coloured liquor he seemed to enjoy so much. He caught her watching him. 'Would you care for some? It will burn away whatever troubles you.'

She shook her head.

He downed it in one gulp. 'It is not every day I defy my mother,' he explained. 'Not that I am unwilling to do so, but it is generally easier not to. For everyone. She has a way of making someone pay the piper when she does not get her own way. Very likely you will suffer.'

Mary Margaret gaped at him. She had not realised he knew how his mother behaved. For some reason, she had thought him blind to the Countess's faults. Most people seemed not to see the uncomfortable in those they loved. Emily certainly could not see the evil in Thomas, or if she did she refused to admit it. Even when he hit her she made excuses. Ravensford made none for his mother.

He gave her a devilish smile that made her knees weaken. 'Please be seated, Miss O'Brien. I won't bite. I have never bitten an unwilling woman.'

She dropped into the nearest chair, shocked by what he had said. 'I hope not.'

He laughed wryly. 'What are you afraid of, Miss O'Brien? That I will ask you to be my mistress again? Don't worry. Even I understand no when it has been said to me twice.'

'You treat this with levity, but I am appalled at all you have bought. I said the one dress, not an entire wardrobe. What will people think?'

He poured himself another glass of liquor and downed it in one long swallow. Putting the empty glass down, he studied her with a reckless air. 'Who gives a damn, Miss O'Brien? Surely you don't.'

She sputtered. How could he think that? 'Just because I am not Quality does not mean I don't value my reputation. In truth, I need to be more careful than one of your station. If I become ruined, true or not, I will never be allowed to make my living. No one will have me in their household.'

'You are right as far as it goes,' he drawled. He poured another drink and downed it as quickly as he had the last. 'However, if I give you a letter of recommendation then you will get work.'

'Who made you all powerful?' she demanded, incensed by his arrogance. 'I very much doubt that a letter from the Prince Regent would negate the rumours that will fly about your buying me a complete wardrobe.'

He bowed to her. 'Then we shall put it to the test if need be.'

She gaped at him. 'You would get the Prince of Wales to write a letter about this? You are mad.'

He eyed her speculatively. 'There are moments when I have thought so. Particularly lately.'

His words nonplussed her. She had a strange feeling that he meant more than he said. It was time she was gone even if he had not dismissed her. She stood.

'I have not given you permission to leave, Miss O'Brien.' Keeping his gaze on her, he poured himself another drink and downed it just as quickly.

She frowned at him. 'I doubt you are capable, my lord. You are guzzling that vile stuff as though it were water.'

He poured another glass and saluted her with it. 'This is the finest Irish whiskey. You should be proud of your country. I brought this back when we came from my mother's. A friend first introduced me to this drink, only his is Scotch.'

He gulped the golden liquid down, his Adam's apple moving in rhythm with the whiskey. She winced. No wonder he was acting so strangely. He had to be the worse for drink.

'I will send back everything but the one dress.' She turned and made for the door. Enough was enough.

'Miss O'Brien,' he said, his voice a silky threat, 'I still have not dismissed you. Had you forgotten?'

She paused and looked back and gasped. He was right behind her; the sound of his movement had been muffled by the thick carpet. He grabbed her left wrist and held it tightly so that she could not get away without squirming. She stood like a statue.

'You are not yourself, my lord.' She hoped her voice sounded more firm to him than it did to her.

He grinned wolfishly. 'If you are implying that I am drunk, you are correct. However, I think…' he pulled her closer '…I am more myself than I have ever been around you.'

Before she realised it was happening, her body was flush to his. His face was scant inches above hers. And his mouth was a breath away from hers. Her eyes widened as his intention became clear.

'Adding insult to injury, my lord?' she managed to say before his lips found hers.

'Pleasure to inclination,' he murmured against her flesh. 'Close your eyes, Miss O'Brien.'

Too late. She had waited too long to struggle. His arms slid around her waist, trapping her hands against his chest. She pushed but to no avail. She was held tightly and expertly.

His mouth met hers in a rush of heat that left her feeling bewildered and delighted. She tingled from her lips to her toes. His tongue slid along her skin, tickling her into a gasp. He darted in, flicking against her teeth. In her surprise, she nearly bit him.

'Ouch,' he said, drawing out and looking down at her. 'You aren't supposed to do that.'

All she could do was stare at him.

'Let's try this again,' he murmured.

'I won't. That is—'

'Hush.'

His mouth moved against hers in seductive abandon. His tongue pressed for entry, then darted in and melded with hers. He tasted of heather and smoke and something infinitely sweet. Heat, then cold, then shivers raced through her body. She felt like she was falling into an abyss from which she would never be able to escape. Her entire world exploded and then came back together with him at the centre.

His mouth broke from hers only to nuzzle the

tender spot just below her ear. His hands roamed her back, stroking muscles that had tightened in delight. He moulded her to his desire. She moaned.

His lips returned to hers just as one of his hands slid to her breast and cupped it. The combination was too much. She arched into his caress. She returned his kiss as passionately as he gave it. She thought she would die if he quit. She purred.

When he broke away, she was stunned. He held her to him, but his hands dropped to her waist, his forehead rested on hers.

'I want you,' he murmured, his voice a husky rasp.

Bewilderment held her motionless in his arms. Her breathing was rapid and shallow. She felt bereft.

'Mary Margaret. Sweetheart,' he whispered against her cheek where he nuzzled her. 'You can't know how long I have wanted to do that.'

His hands shifted to rub up and down her back, fitting her against his enflamed body. She didn't know where she ended and he began. Her senses were in a daze of desire. The knowledge of his power over her was frightening, so much so that she snapped back to reality.

'Oh, no,' she moaned, appalled at what she had just done.

She pushed hard against him. This time he had

not been expecting resistance and his grip failed. She stumbled from his embrace, panting as though she had run up a flight of stairs. He moved to take her back into his arms and she scrambled behind the chair where she had so recently sat.

'No! We cannot, that is I cannot, that is—'

'Cannot kiss? Make love?' He watched her with tender amusement. 'Why not?'

'You are drunk,' she gasped. 'How can you say such things?'

He sighed and ran his fingers through his hair. 'Probably. Although not so much that I don't know what I am doing.'

'What if someone came in and saw us? Especially after what you have already done.'

'Is that all you can think about—what other people will say? I have wanted to kiss and caress you since the instant I first heard your throaty purr. You excited me then and you excite me now.'

She fought back the delight his words created. To know that he had been attracted to her from the beginning was heady stuff. The interest she had felt was not all one-sided. And yet, what did this really mean? Nothing. He was treating her as he would a mistress. The momentary madness ended.

'How could you?' she demanded, fighting back the tears that threatened. He was attracted to her, desired her, but that was all this was to him. A physical liaison that any woman could satisfy.

'I could because you wanted me to.'

She gasped. 'I am not a loose woman.'

His eyes narrowed. 'I never said you were.'

She put a hand to her chest, wishing her heartbeat would return to normal. 'But you are treating me as one. The dresses and…and the kiss and…'

He took a step toward her. 'Then marry me.'

She gasped. Shame engulfed her. 'How dare you insult me? You don't mean that. I won't play your game.'

He took another step forward and reached for her. She darted to the right, narrowly escaping him.

'You play the game, Miss O'Brien. Not I. Hot, then cold, but never consistent.'

Fury made her bold. 'I think not.'

Before he could try to catch her again, she bolted for the door and through into the hall. She didn't look back and didn't slow down until she was safe in her room.

Ravensford watched her flee. What had he done, proposing to her? It was the last thing he had intended when she entered the library. But the whiskey, his pent-up desire, her ardent response to his lovemaking…everything had conspired to make him act less than judiciously.

He twisted around and went to pour another drink. In for a penny, in for a pound. He downed two more glasses of the potent liquor until he was well and truly foxed.

A knock on the door was followed by the butler's discreet entrance. 'My lord, the Earl of Perth is here.'

Ravensford turned from his vacant study of the garden. 'Send him in.'

Seconds later Perth entered, one dark brow raised. 'You look the worse for wear, old man.'

'Have a drink?'

Perth grinned. 'Is that the cause or only the solution?'

Ravensford pointedly turned his back and poured two drinks. Facing his friend again, he handed Perth one glass.

'To lust in all its forms,' Ravensford said, toasting Perth.

Perth chuckled. 'A mistress or Miss O'Brien?'

Ravensford downed his drink. 'Oh, Miss O'Brien, who else? That woman has been the bane of my existence since I met her.'

'Following in Brabourne's footsteps?' Perth drank his whiskey more slowly, amusement lightening his swarthy complexion.

'Nothing of the sort. At least, not exactly.' Ravensford sank into a chair and motioned for

Perth to do the same. 'Brabourne married for love.
I might do it for desire. Can't love a woman who
is planning to steal from m'mother. No matter if
m'mother deserves to have her jewels stolen or
not.'

Perth laughed. 'Your speech is as disorganised
as your mother's always is. I swear there are a few
pieces of this puzzle missing.'

'Damn,' Ravensford said, appalled that he was
slipping into his mother's habit. ''Tis a long story.'

'I have the time if you have more whiskey.'

'Right.'

Ravensford got the decanter and set it between
them. In succinct sentences he told Perth everything.

'Don't you think marriage is a drastic solution?'
Perth finally asked.

'Undoubtedly.' Ravensford tipped the decanter
up only to see it was empty. 'Jones,' he bellowed.

The butler poked his head in. 'Yes, my lord?'

'More whiskey.'

Within minutes they were re-supplied.

'Blasted woman does things to my mind, not to
mention my body,' Ravensford explained. 'The
words were out of my mouth before I knew they
were said.'

'And they cannot be taken back. You are a gentleman, unlike myself.'

Ravensford leaned over and poured Perth more whiskey, narrowly missing the table. 'You are too hard on yourself, Perth. Your code of honour is as well honed as anyone's. You just think it isn't.'

A dark look settled over Perth's features. 'So you say.' He gulped his drink. 'Come, White's beckons. I have an itch to gamble.'

Thankful to be gone from the turmoil he knew roiled upstairs, Ravensford called for his great coat, hat and cane. Neither man cared that it was only late afternoon as they strolled from the house and made their way to Bond Street.

Upstairs, Mary Margaret was stunned by the amount of clothing Ravensford had purchased. Boxes and dresses covered her bed, the two chairs and every other inch of space. Silks, cottons, taffetas, wools—every fabric imaginable, in all the colours of the rainbow, deluged her room. Then there were shoes and bonnets for every imaginable occasion. He had spent a fortune on her. She would never be able to repay him.

Why had he done this? Anger bubbled up in her.

'Ohh, Mary Margaret,' Annabell's light voice said in awe.

Mary Margaret turned around, tamping down on her fury. There was no reason to take her anger at

Ravensford out on Annabell. 'I didn't hear you enter.'

Annabell grinned. 'I knocked. When you didn't answer, I came in.' Her gaze skimmed the room. 'I can understand why you didn't hear me. If I had just received all of this, I would be oblivious to the world too.'

Mary Margaret frowned. 'It will all have to go back. I cannot afford it. I told the Earl I would take the one dress. Never this.'

'You cannot return all of this,' Annabell said, horrified. 'What will Ravensford say? What will the servants say if they see all these boxes going out?'

'What will they say if the boxes stay here?' Mary Margaret could not keep the bitterness from her words. 'I don't care what Ravensford thinks. He is too domineering by half.'

Annabell shrugged. 'He is a man and an Earl. He cannot help himself.'

'So true,' Mary Margaret said. 'So disgustingly true.'

Chapter Twelve

Mary Margaret sat demurely in one of her old dresses and watched as the Countess and Annabell entertained Mr Finch. The Countess poured tea and dispensed sandwiches with a blithe disregard for Mary Margaret. She was not surprised. For the last three days, the Countess had been doing everything in her power to make her miserable.

She wanted to burn every piece of clothing Ravensford had foisted on her. And she would when this farce was done. Right now she was only grateful that the hateful man had not come near her since his mockery of a proposal. His absence had nearly convinced her that he regretted making such game of her, for she never doubted that the offer was made in spite over her rejection of his previous overtures.

The Countess glanced her way with a malicious

smile. Mary Margaret turned her head to keep the older woman from seeing the anger and resentment in her eyes. Not even the serene beauty of the rose garden could ease her turbulent emotions. She was sorely tempted to ask permission to be excused even though she knew the Countess would refuse.

'My lady,' the butler intoned, 'the Reverend Mr Fox.'

Fear speared Mary Margaret, leaving her breathless and clammy. It *had* been him at the theatre, just as she had feared. He had come to London to spy on her, but why was he here? He could not talk to her in front of everyone, at least not about stealing the Countess's jewellery.

'Ah, Mr Fox,' the Countess said coolly. 'What brings you to London? I fear your flock will be lost without your guiding hand.'

He laughed as though at a great witticism and advanced into the room despite the lukewarm reception. 'You are always so droll, my lady. I found that I missed your intelligence and beauty.'

Mary Margaret watched in awe as the Countess began to visibly thaw. Thomas had that way with women. To her horror, Annabell gazed at her brother-in-law as though she beheld a god. Her stomach started churning.

From the corner of his eye, Thomas slid his blue

gaze over her. She knew that look well, and it boded no good. She had to do something.

Surging to her feet, she said, 'Oh, Thomas, have you brought me a message from Emily?'

He gloated at her. 'She sends her love and hopes you will return soon.'

'I miss her awfully.'

That was true and there was nothing else she could say. It would only inflame the Countess more if she professed to want to return home. But she knew that Thomas was telling her to get the job done.

Dismissing her, Thomas focussed his attention on Annabell. 'Miss Winston, I trust you are enjoying your stay in London.'

Annabell beamed up at him, the dimple in her right cheek peeking out. 'Immensely.'

He bowed over her extended hand. 'I never doubted it with the Countess showing you about.'

Mary Margaret's initial fear abated as she listened to Thomas's effusive charm. She wondered why the two women did not see through him. But then, she had not at first. She, like they, had been entranced by his spectacular good looks and easy way with words.

'Very prettily done,' Ravensford's baritone said from the doorway.

He had entered while all of them had been focussed on Thomas. His cynical gaze rested on her brother-in-law, and Mary Margaret's receding fear began to return. There was something about the way Ravensford held himself that spelled danger. Perhaps his broad shoulders were a bit too straight, or his square jaw too tight. She was not sure exactly what the change was, but she knew him well enough by now to know that he did not like Thomas.

Her initial unease was increased tenfold when Ravensford's glance passed over her. Dark circles intensified the colour of his eyes. He looked debauched and deadly, as she imaged a man would look who has reached the end of his tolerance. Surely Thomas's presence had not caused this condition. She devoutly hoped it had nothing to do with their confrontation in the library either.

'Ahem... I must be leaving,' Mr Finch said, breaking into the silence.

They had all forgotten him. Now everyone concentrated on his departure, using action to ease the discomfort caused by Ravensford's presence.

'I shall be sure and keep a dance for you,' Annabell said, referring to Finch's earlier request for a waltz at her coming-out ball.

He took her proffered hand and gushed, 'I shall hold my breath until then.'

It was all Mary Margaret could do not to laugh at his dramatisation.

'Then you will be in no shape for the dance,' Ravensford said drily.

Mr Finch looked like a balloon that the air had been let out of. 'Very practical, my lord.'

'Upon occasion I try to do the mundane.'

Mary Margaret listened to Ravensford in surprise. She had never seen him jab at someone before. Something was bothering him.

Mr Finch took his leave and hurried from the room. Ravensford settled himself comfortably in one of the chairs, his left leg over the right. His Hessians shone like mirrors.

'What brings you all the way to London, Mr Fox?'

Mary Margaret watched Thomas smile benignly at the Earl. 'My father is here for the Season and I am come to pay my respects.'

Ravensford quirked one brow.

The Countess asked point-blank, 'Is your father in trade, Mr Fox?'

Mary Margaret would have laughed if she could not see how furious Thomas was at the slight. His blue eyes were hard chips. His finely wrought mouth was a thin slash. Somehow, he managed to keep his tone level, even light.

'No, my lady. My father is Viscount Fox.' He

flashed a false smile around the room. 'I am a younger son.'

A considering light entered Ravensford's eyes, turning them to the bright colour of emerald with the sun shining through. 'And went into the clergy instead of the army.'

Thomas turned to face Ravensford directly. 'My middle brother is in the army.'

'Why, I didn't know you were related to old Fox,' the Countess said. 'How delightful. You must come to Annabell's ball this Thursday. I am sure we sent your father an invitation.' She turned her sharp gaze on Mary Margaret. 'Didn't we?'

She nodded, remembering the name. It had struck her that it was the same as Thomas's, but she had not considered that his father might be in London. What a very small world the aristocracy was.

'I—' Thomas said.

Ravensford spoke smoothly over Thomas. 'I am sure that a man of the cloth, as Mr Fox is, would find our entertaining too hedonistic.' The smile he turned on Thomas didn't reach his eyes. 'We would not want to make him uncomfortable.'

Mary Margaret enjoyed Ravensford's needling of Thomas, knowing her brother-in-law was too far from home to take his fury out on Emily. Still, part of her dreaded what he would do when he returned to Ireland. Or when he finally demanded a meeting with her.

Thomas gave Ravensford a bland look. 'I should be delighted to attend Miss Winston's ball. I am sure she will put every other young lady in the shade.' He gave the Countess and Annabell a brilliant smile.

Mary Margaret twisted away to look anywhere but at Thomas, but not before she saw the disgust Ravensford did nothing to hide. The Countess and Annabell, however, were enchanted.

'In that case,' Ravensford drawled, rising, 'we will expect you after dinner.'

Disappointment flashed across Thomas's face and Mary Margaret realised that he had been hoping for an invitation to dinner before the ball. She breathed a sigh of relief that Ravensford had prevented that. She did not want to see Thomas any more than she had to.

To add insult to injury, Ravensford added, 'Mother, aren't you and Annabell expected at Mrs Bridges' this afternoon?'

'Goodness, I had completely forgotten.' The Countess rose and motioned to Annabell. 'We must change and be on our way.' She held a hand out to Thomas, who took it and raised it to his lips. 'We shall expect you on Thursday.'

He bowed and took his leave without even glancing at Mary Margaret. She relaxed.

'Is he the curate who introduced you to my mother? The one who is married to your sister?'

She started. In her relief at having Thomas gone, she had forgotten how acute Ravensford was. Particularly when no one else was around and he could say what he wished.

'Yes.'

'Do you know him well?'

Apprehension and guilt made their way into her thoughts. Why was he asking these questions? What did it matter to him?

'Better than I would like.'

'And why is that?'

His eyes held hers. She wondered again how much he knew. Very likely more than she wished.

She chose her words carefully. 'He is not always as charming with women as he was this afternoon.'

'How is that?'

He evinced only mild curiosity, but Mary Margaret sensed something deeper. Her shoulders tightened.

'Oh, just…just that I have seen him lose his temper upon occasion. That is all.'

Disgust at herself twisted her mouth. Now she was being like Emily and evading the real question. Why did they protect Thomas?

'I see.'

She looked sharply at him. He watched her with narrowed eyes. She could almost think he did see.

'Does he visit London often?'

She licked dry lips. 'Not that I know of.'

'Does he visit his father's estate?'

'Is this an interrogation, my lord?' She was on the defensive and knew it. What did he want from her? 'I do not keep track of Thomas's comings and goings.'

He took out his pocket watch and checked the time. 'Perhaps he is here because of you?'

'I don't see why,' she answered without thinking.

'He must be concerned about your welfare. You are his wife's sister and he did find you employment with my mother, as awful as that is.'

'Well, perhaps,' she murmured, realising belatedly that he had given her a perfectly plausible reason for Thomas being in London. Along with his family being here.

'Then he will accept an invitation to accompany us to Astley's Amphitheatre tomorrow?'

'No. That is, I mean, he surely would, but we are not going there tomorrow. Annabell wants to see the wild animals in the Tower.'

His gaze on her was sardonic. 'Then Mr Fox

will join us for a tour of the Tower. I will have my secretary send him around an invitation.'

She gulped back a retort. The last thing she wanted was to have Thomas with them. But she had no control over who Ravensford invited. She could not even stop him from buying her a complete wardrobe.

'And about the clothes you bought for me, my lord. What do you suggest I wear to the Tower?'

His eyes narrowed at the sarcasm in her voice. She was even surprised by her daring to take him to task. The surprise was quickly followed by worry as she realised that in order to be comfortable enough to berate him, however so slightly, she must be *very* used to his company.

'Wear whatever you want, Miss O'Brien. Except for Annabell's ball. Then I want you to wear the pink dress Madame Bertrice altered for you.'

She made him a mock curtsy. 'And we both know that I will do as you bid, my lord. You schooled me in obeying orders before we ever left Ireland.'

His lips parted in a white slash of teeth. 'So you say, but your actions put the lie to your words.'

Before she could think of something else to say, he rose and sauntered from the room. He was the most infuriating man.

Well, she would get the better of him. Ravensford would find out nothing about her and Thomas because she did not intend to do as Thomas ordered. As for the clothes, she would go straight up to her room and continue folding and repacking them in the boxes she had not let the footmen return to Madame Bertrice.

Mary Margaret held up an afternoon dress of the finest white muslin trimmed with emerald ribbons. Crossing to the mirror, she held the frock up to her face and could not help but admire the picture. The garment was perfect for her.

She sighed and turned away. Temptation. She was not keeping these clothes no matter how beautiful they made her look. She was not so vain as to risk her reputation further.

A knock on her door was followed by Annabell's entrance. She and the Countess must have just returned from their afternoon visit to Mrs Bridges. The girl sat on the bed and watched Mary Margaret fold the afternoon dress.

'Ravensford will be furious,' Annabell said.

'Then he should not do something as disreputable as buying his mother's companion a complete wardrobe.' In a fit of pique, she stuffed the folded garment into too small a space.

Annabell giggled, then became suddenly silent. Mary Margaret frowned at the wadded-up gown before looking at her charge. A dreamy look transformed the girl's features.

'What did you think of Mr Fox?'

Unease crept down Mary Margaret's back. The look on Annabell's face screamed trouble.

'Annabell, Thomas is married to my younger sister, Emily.'

She hoped her tone had been pragmatic with just a hint of sympathy. It was so hard to tell how one really sounded, especially to a young woman who had just been smitten by a very handsome man.

'Oh,' Annabell said lightly. 'What are you doing to that beautiful dress?'

Mary Margaret scowled. 'I am trying to repack it.'

'I will send my maid in to help you,' Annabell said. 'It will take you hours to do this by yourself.'

'Thank you, but I can manage.'

Mary Margaret had no intention of getting anyone else into trouble with the Earl. When he started raving about the clothes being returned, she would be the only person responsible.

'As you wish,' Annabell said.

Mary Margaret gave the girl a considering look. Annabell was too docile. Normally she would have argued with Mary Margaret about the use of her personal maid.

The disquiet that had surfaced at Annabell's

mention of Thomas returned. Mary Margaret knew only too well how devastatingly attractive her brother-in-law was to women.

The next day Mary Margaret watched anxiously as Thomas took Annabell to see the lions, who numbered among the many wild animals housed at the Tower. The girl was smitten and Thomas was doing everything in his power to keep her that way. It did not help matters that the Countess had stayed home as usual. Had she come, Thomas would have been forced to divide his charms between the two women. As it was, he could focus completely on Annabell. She had to catch up with them.

Even worried as she was, she sensed Ravensford's presence before he spoke. Her skin tingled and her senses sharpened. He did that to her.

'Is something bothering you?'

'No. Should something be?' She immediately regretted the answer. She owed it to him and to Annabell to bring her concern into the open. 'That is not true.' She sighed. 'I am worried about Annabell. I think she is more interested in Thomas than is proper.'

'He is married to your sister.'

'Yes. That is why I am so concerned about Annabell.'

'I should have thought your sister would take first priority.'

What to tell him without telling him the truth? This was so hard. She shook her head. How could Emily stand the constant lying and subterfuge needed to protect Thomas's reputation? And yet, here she was hedging. She was not strong enough to tell anyone about the beating. Nor would most people care. Under the law, Emily was Thomas's to deal with as he pleased.

Instead she implied something else. 'My sister is used to Thomas's ways.'

Ravensford watched the couple disappear around one of the buildings. 'So theirs was not a love match.'

'It was for her,' Mary Margaret said in a tiny voice.

'Ahh. I am sorry for her.'

She searched his face for the truth of his feelings. 'I believe you really are. But aren't most marriages made for convenience?'

'Most. My parents' was a love match. It just so happened that both families approved.' He shrugged. 'And sometimes arranged marriages become ones of love.'

'But that does not protect Annabell from Thomas's charms.'

He rubbed the sapphire in his signet ring, a habit

she realised he had when he was troubled. 'You speak as though you expect Thomas to take advantage of her. Isn't that a rather harsh judgement to make against anyone and particularly a man of the cloth?'

Still more subterfuge, and yet Thomas did flirt with women. She was never sure if he went further.

She shrugged. 'Perhaps. I just don't want to see Annabell hurt.'

'Then we had best catch up with them.'

She sighed in relief.

Ravensford was now positive that Thomas had been the man threatening Mary Margaret, and his power had to do with her sister, Emily. He watched her as they searched for the other couple. There was a worried crease in her broad forehead and a pinched look around her mouth. She truly was concerned.

He saw Thomas's blond hair before he saw Annabell. Instead of going to the lions, the two had stopped to look at the ravens. It was said that if the ravens ever left the Tower, the monarchy would fall. A nice legend. He was more interested in the fact that Annabell clung to Thomas, her face radiant as she laughed at something he was saying. He began to understand why Mary Margaret did not like this situation.

Mary Margaret picked up speed and he put out

a hand to slow her. When she looked back at him, an irritated frown replacing the worry, he shook his head. He forced her to saunter up with him as though they had no care in the world.

'I thought you two were going to the lions?' he drawled.

Annabell beamed. 'We are, but Thomas was just entertaining me with stories of his parish. He is so droll.'

The man could even look modest, Ravensford saw in disgust. 'How interesting.'

Thomas gave Ravensford a challenging smile. 'Miss Winston has invited me to go to Astley's Amphitheatre tomorrow, Ravensford. I hope that will be all right with you and the Countess.'

Ravensford returned the smile. 'Of course. Perth is going so we shall be a party.' Perth did not know he was going.

For the rest of the afternoon, Ravensford kept with the couple. He had not liked Thomas Fox the first time he had seen him. There was something about the man that offended. The feeling was strengthened by the knowledge that, although Mary Margaret was careful about what she said, he knew she felt the same way. And Thomas had ordered her to steal from his mother. It would be his very great pleasure to catch the scoundrel. The problem would be to keep Mary Margaret from being implicated.

He glanced at her. She watched Thomas with an anxious look in her eyes that made him want to gather her close and tell her everything would be fine. He would protect her.

He shook his head. First he had asked her to be his mistress, then his wife. He was not in the market for either. If his luck held, she would continue to refuse him on both offers. Or so he told himself.

Chapter Thirteen

Descending the stairs, Mary Margaret saw that Perth had already arrived and Annabell was champing at the bit to be off. The girl had been in a dither all day, picking first one gown and then discarding it in favour of another. She acted as though she were meeting a lover. The idea was enough to make Mary Margaret's blood run cold.

'I am sorry I am late.'

She did not explain that there had been a stain on her best gown so she had been forced to change at the last moment. She might not have nice clothes, but she had clean ones.

Ravensford scowled at her. She returned his look with a bland one. She knew without his saying a word that he was irritated that she was not wearing one of Madame Bertrice's gowns. Well, let him stew in his juices. She tossed her head, realising belatedly that the movement lost most of its defiance when there was no hair to swing. As usual, her hair was in a tight chignon.

'We had best be going,' Perth said, 'before Annabell here wears a hole in her slippers with all the shuffling she is doing.' He grinned mockingly at her. 'I did not know that beautiful women riding bareback on trained horses excited you.' He cast a wicked glance at Ravensford. 'I would not have been surprised if Ravensford was the one dancing about. He has always had a penchant for exotic women.'

From the way Ravensford ignored his friend's barb, Mary Margaret decided the taunt had gone wide of the Earl only to hit her square in the heart. Just the thought of Ravensford looking longingly at another woman was enough to make her chest tighten painfully. Now it seemed she was going to have to actually see him desiring other women. She felt sick.

If she did not have to go along as Annabell's chaperon, she would plead a headache or anything to get out of this excursion. As it was, the Countess had already beaten her to the excuse.

The ride to Westminster Bridge Road, where the theatre was, seemed to last forever. She said little as Perth continued to tease Annabell and tried to goad Ravensford. Annabell rose magnificently to the occasion, while Ravensford remained a stoic.

'You are in rare form tonight, Perth,' Ravensford said. 'Is there something about this outing that you have failed to tell me?'

A gleam entered Perth's dark eyes but his voice was noncommittal. 'A mild diversion, nothing more. You shall see.'

The carriage halted and the gentlemen exited. This time Perth helped Mary Margaret out. She put her hand in his, not surprised when she felt nothing but the strength of his fingers. She refused to let herself feel disappointment that Ravensford had helped Annabell. The less interaction she had with him the better for her peace of mind and body.

Thomas waited for them at the door.

As before, he was impeccably dressed. Mary Margaret marvelled that her brother-in-law could dress in the height of male fashion, yet live in a cottage no better than that of a prosperous farmer. Viscount Fox must be supplying his son.

The five of them exchanged greetings and entered the theatre. Mary Margaret had known the place would be large, but this was magnificent. Boxes went up four stories on three sides. The fourth side contained a stage and the orchestra. A huge chandelier cast enough light to make it possible to see across the rink where a scantily clad woman was standing on the back of a prancing horse and playing a tambourine.

She must have gaped for Ravensford said drily, 'It can be overwhelming the first time.'

All she could do was nod.

Ravensford led them to a box he had reserved while Perth made his way around the perimeter. Mary Margaret was entranced before they even sat down. She marvelled at the acts of equestrian daring. Beside her, Annabell clapped and joined the crowd in showing their appreciation.

'So,' Ravensford murmured under his breath.

Mary Margaret was so attuned to him that she heard even though she knew he had not meant her to. Turning to him, she saw he had a knowing smile and his attention was not on the performance, but intent on someone in a booth across the rink.

Perth—and a woman. He bowed over her hand as she smiled up at him. Even from this distance, Mary Margaret could make out hair the colour of spun silver. And she had to be wearing a king's ransom in jewels for she sparkled like the chandelier.

'Who is she?' she asked softly.

'Lady de Lisle, one of Perth's old flirts.' He frowned as Perth left the woman's side. 'What is he up to now? She broke with him many years ago and married another man. He has never forgiven her.'

'He seems to have forgiven her quite well,' Mary Margaret said with only a hint of sarcasm.

'He is up to something.'

'Perhaps he still cares for her.'

'I think not. He did not take kindly to being left at the altar while she ran away with another man.'

Mary Margaret gasped and waited for him to elaborate, but he did not. Not even when Perth joined them and sat down on the other side of Annabell. She did note that periodically Lady de Lisle glanced their way. Perth did not return the look.

At the intermission, Thomas rose and said, 'Mary Margaret, come with me for a breath of air. I have news from home.' He bowed to the others. 'If you will excuse us, this is of a personal nature.'

Apprehension made her shudder. He was going to tell her that her time was up. She rose, feeling like a prisoner going to her execution, and followed him from the theatre.

Outside he dropped the pose of solicitous brother-in-law and his voice turned hard. 'Have you got the jewels yet? I warn you, my patience is not endless.'

Her hands felt like ice even in the gloves she wore. Thank goodness he was here and Emily was in Ireland. Knowing that her sister was safe gave her the bravado she needed.

'I must have more time. Just until Annabell's ball.' She took a deep breath and rushed on. 'While everyone is busy I will sneak up to the Countess's room and steal the jewels. No one will expect it.'

His fingers tightened cruelly on her arm. 'Be sure that you do so. I will expect you to pass them to me that night.'

'Oh, no, someone might see. 'Twould be better to meet you the next day.'

But she would not do so. The day of the ball was quarter's day and she would have her pay. She would be off for Ireland. How, she did not know, but she would manage. She knew the way Ravensford had travelled. She would take the coach and the ferry.

'Don't try to trick me, Mary Margaret. I will make you sorry if you do.'

His grip was so tight she knew she would have bruises the next day. They would be worth it for the knowledge that she had outsmarted him.

'This appears to be a very serious discussion,' Ravensford said, walking toward them.

Mary Margaret jumped, wrenching her arm painfully when Thomas did not release her. Thomas stood calmly.

He smiled smoothly. 'We are just finished, Ravensford. I fear my news was not all good. Mary Margaret's sister has an inflammation of the lungs. Fortunately, the vicar's good wife is caring for her in my absence. Still, it is never comforting to know your loved ones are in danger.'

Mary Margaret heard the implied threat, but there was nothing she could say.

'I am sorry to hear that,' Ravensford said. He took Mary Margaret's unresisting hand and pulled her from Thomas's grip. 'Would you like me to arrange for my mother's doctor to see her?'

Mary Margaret looked into his eyes and saw a strange light in them, as though he waited expectantly for her to say something to him that he already knew. She shook herself at the fancifulness. He was being kind.

'Thank you, my lord.'

'That won't be necessary, Ravensford,' Thomas said curtly. 'My wife is well cared for.'

Ravensford gave the other man a cutting look. 'I did not ask you, Fox.'

Mary Margaret cringed and wished herself anywhere but between these two men. She did not think Emily was sick, or hoped that if she truly was Thomas would have told her before Ravensford's arrival. But then, neither of them had expected the Earl.

Concern for Emily grew. She glanced at

Thomas's furious face. To defy him would only make matters worse, and yet Emily must be her first concern. While the vicar's wife was a good woman, she was not a doctor. She would ask Ravensford to send his physician when they were away from Thomas.

'Thomas is probably right, my lord. The vicar's wife is very good with the sick.'

Ravensford gave her a look of disgust. 'As you wish, Miss O'Brien.'

She wanted to cringe from his disapproval but knew that would only make him despise her cowardice more. Meekly, she allowed him to lead her back inside the theatre.

She studiously avoided looking at Ravensford for the remainder of their stay. Even after Thomas made his farewells, she kept as far from the Earl as Annabell and Perth's presence allowed. At the town house, she kept her head down and mumbled a 'thank you' when Perth helped her out of the carriage.

'My pleasure,' he murmured sardonically.

She gave him a sharp glance but said nothing. As soon as Annabell was safely tucked away she would search out Ravensford and ask him to send the doctor to Emily. In the meantime he would have to continue thinking badly of her.

Ravensford watched Mary Margaret enter the

foyer behind Annabell, disgusted with the way she had let Thomas dictate to her.

'If the sky looked like your face,' Perth observed drily, 'we would be in for the storm of the century. Come to White's and tell me on the way what Miss O'Brien has done this time.'

'Good idea,' he muttered, pivoting sharply and re-entering the carriage. Inside he succinctly told Perth about the incident with Thomas and the doctor.

'Come along, old man,' Perth said as they reached White's. 'You need diversion.'

As they entered the exclusive men's club a silence fell on the room. Ravensford looked around, noting the familiar faces. Most occupants nodded; a few would not meet his gaze. A single man rose and came toward him.

'Wondered when word would reach you, Ravensford,' the lone man said. Tall and thin, he moved gracefully. Full grey hair swept back from a high forehead and black brows. Ebony eyes calmly studied Ravensford, as though the man searched for signs of agitation.

Ravensford raised one brow. 'What word was that, Chillings?'

Chillings looked at Perth. 'Do you know?'

Perth shook his head. 'We just came from Astley's Amphitheatre. Needed some normality.'

A tiny, feral smile revealed Viscount Chillings's teeth. 'Seems someone has it in for you, Ravensford. I wonder if it is the same person who wrote in the betting book about Brabourne.'

Ravensford stiffened. His and Perth's friend, the Duke of Brabourne, had found a damaging remark in White's famous betting book about the woman he was now married to. The comment had precipitated Brabourne's proposal. For the Duke it had been the best thing. He and his wife had a love match.

Without a word, Ravensford strode to where the book was kept. He opened it to the last page and read: What Earl, known for his prowess with the fairer sex, has bought his mother's companion an entire wardrobe? Beneath the damaging words was a record of the bets placed on when the companion would be leaving the Countess and moving into her own establishment, paid for by the Earl.

He had not expected this. He had told Madame Bertrice that if she valued his patronage no word would get out of who had paid for Mary Margaret's clothes. As far as the world was concerned, his mother had been the provider. This put paid to all his careful planning.

Mary Margaret was ruined, just as she had feared. With this circulating, she would not be allowed into the homes of any woman of the *ton*. Her use as a chaperon for Annabell was over.

'Easy, old man,' Perth murmured, putting a firm hand on Ravensford's stiff shoulder. 'Seems someone is out to get you the same way Brabourne was got. Although it didn't do him any harm,' he ended with a wicked smile. 'Much the contrary.'

'Brabourne was in love. I am not,' Ravensford hissed for Perth's ears only.

Chillings, his task done, rejoined his group. For a moment Ravensford wondered if the Viscount had written the damaging words. He as quickly dismissed them. He barely knew Chillings and there was no bad blood between them.

Ravensford looked slowly around the room, meeting gazes when possible. The fury that rode him abated enough that he could contemplate murder calmly. Whoever had done this would pay.

They left without a word to anyone. Outside, Ravensford pounded his cane against the ground.

'Blast it to hell! Whoever did this will pay.'

'Just as he did when this was done to Brabourne?'

Ravensford scowled at Perth. 'Brabourne never found the scoundrel, but working together he and I will now.'

They continued walking, having waved off the

carriage. The cool air helped Ravensford's temper, but did not erase it.

'In the meantime,' Perth drawled, 'there are several things you can do.'

'Such as?'

'Send the chit back to Ireland or set her up in her own establishment as the mysterious writer suggests.'

'She is not my mistress,' Ravensford said through clenched teeth.

'But not for lack of interest on your part,' Perth said.

There was no answer so he gave none.

Perth left him at his town house door. 'Tell your mother that I will be at Annabell's ball tomorrow, will you? I forgot to send my acceptance.'

'You are the most irresponsible scoundrel,' Ravensford said without malice. 'Yet you are invited everywhere.'

'It must be my charm,' Perth drawled sardonically. 'It cannot be because of my title and wealth.'

'Absolutely not. Especially with Lady de Lisle. She was an heiress in her own right and old de Lisle left her very nicely provided for.' He gave his friend a knowing look which Perth ignored.

'I believe I will call in on an establishment we both know,' Perth said with an air of mild interest. 'Care to join me?'

He was fleetingly tempted. But then a face formed in his mind's eye: green eyes, ebony hair and lips he had tasted twice and wanted to taste more. No, until he was through this attraction to Mary Margaret O'Brien, no other woman interested him in the slightest. Probably he would not even be able to perform. That would make the betting book and then things would be a thousand times worse than the mess they already were.

'No,' he told Perth. 'I have much to do tomorrow. Some of us have responsibilities.'

Perth chuckled as he sauntered away.

Ravensford climbed the steps and took his key out. The door opened. Timothy, the youngest footman, stood carefully erect but his eyes were red and half-shut.

Ravensford sighed in exasperation. 'How many times must I tell Jones not to have you wait up for me? Go to bed.'

Timothy, his face now as red as his eyes, bowed before hurrying off. Ravensford instantly regretted his harsh words. He needed to speak with Jones again, not berate Timothy. The lad only did as ordered.

He took off his beaver hat and gloves, tossed them on the side table, and then propped his cane against the wall. He was exhausted and frustrated.

Something had to be done about Mary Margaret, and he did not like any of his choices.

Mounting the stairs, he did not see the shadow on the second floor landing until he was upon her.

'What the—?'

'My lord. Ravensford,' Mary Margaret whispered. 'I need to speak with you.'

Her face was a luminescent oval in the golden light from the single candle he carried. Her eyes were dark pools. She still wore the dowdy dress she had worn earlier. The sight of it increased his irritation.

'My room is two doors down,' he said coldly, wondering if she would go there.

She nodded. Whatever she needed to tell him must be important. He followed her, curious in spite of himself. She slipped in ahead of him.

He closed the door and stood his ground. When she did not speak for long moments, he said, 'Well?'

Her hands clasped tightly together she said in a tiny voice, 'Will you arrange for your mother's doctor to attend my sister?'

That was the last thing he had expected. 'Braver now that Fox isn't around?'

His voice was harsh as he had meant it to be, but when she took a step back as though he had slapped her he regretted letting his anger come out.

He was not in the habit of intentionally hurting others.

'What could I say? He is her husband.'

'A valid point. Does he often put your sister in jeopardy?'

He watched her closely, hoping she would trust him enough now to tell him the truth. Emotions warred across her face. She looked pinched.

'Sometimes,' she said, her voice a painful rasp.

'Is there something I can help with?'

He took a step toward her. The urge was strong to gather her close and tell her he would protect her and her loved ones from the world. He resisted, even when hope flared briefly in her eyes before dying.

'You still don't trust me,' he said bitterly.

She turned her back to him and he thought he heard a sob. He put the candle down on the nearest table and went to her.

Putting his hands gently on her shoulders, he said, 'Mary Margaret, sweetheart, look at me.'

He felt her stiffen under his touch. She sniffed and raised her head. Hope flared in him.

In a voice that shook only slightly, she said, 'Please let me go. I have told you everything.'

Disappointment speared him, followed by anger. He twirled her around. 'I am fed up with you hedging. The truth is that your brother-in-law does not treat your sister well. He may even beat her and you are afraid for her and of him. I have offered my help. Do you think that I am powerless?'

Her eyes were wide and her mouth an 'O'. 'I... Do you know how hard it is to admit that your sister is beaten whenever her husband is angry? I know it happens, but that does not make it nice.'

He pulled her to him and cupped her head to his chest. Gently he stroked her as he would a cat that had been hurt. He continued, whispering meaningless words until he felt her relax against him.

'I will take care of it,' he promised.

She wriggled her head free and looked up at him. Bewilderment knitted her brows together. 'Why? She is nothing to you. I am nothing to you.'

'How wrong you are,' he murmured. 'How very wrong.'

His kiss was gentle, as though he cherished her above all else. Mary Margaret felt her heart expand with gladness. Perhaps he did care. Perhaps he even loved her. It was a small hope that grew as he tenderly cupped her head and tasted her mouth.

She melted into him, her hands braced against his chest. She felt his heart beat through her fingers, noted that it speeded up as his kiss deepened. She sighed with pleasure.

When one of his hands covered her breast it felt

natural and right. She arched her back to give him better access.

His mouth skimmed over her face and down the side of her neck to the top of her bodice. He licked lightly along the edge of material while he continued to stroke her breast. A sensation of heat and fever started in her abdomen and spread out to every part of her body.

'Turn around,' he murmured, his voice a dark, rich honey.

When she did nothing, just lying in his embrace, he shifted her himself so that the back of her hips were flush to his side. He switched his ministrations to the nape of her neck while his fingers deftly undid the many buttons that held her gown on. A rush of cold hit her as his palms skimmed down her arms, pushing the fabric down.

Slowly, so slowly that she nearly moaned in anticipation, he turned her back around. His eyes held hers captive as his hands slipped inside the bodice of her gown and slid it slowly down her bosom. His flesh burned through her chemise. Her nipples contracted into aching points.

He slid the dress further down. His palms smoothed down her hips and flanks until the gown fell to the floor. She shivered.

His gaze moved to her heaving bosom and lower. 'You are beautiful. Since you fell off the boat, I have wanted to do this. I don't know how I kept from doing this then.' A smile tugged at his lips. 'I am going to make up for all the lost time.'

She heard his words, their meaning penetrating the fog of desire he so easily created in her. This time she did not care. This time she wanted him. She thought he truly wanted her, not just her body. She smiled and moved into his embrace.

He groaned.

He lifted her and carried her to his bed where he carefully laid her on the downy comforter. Her hair had come loose and lay in ebony strands among the pillows.

The light of the candle barely reached them, but he could still see the curves and dark hollows of her body. His own responded with aching quickness. In sure, deft movements, he stripped.

The innocent in Mary Margaret told her to close her eyes. The woman in her kept her gaze focussed on him.

He took her breath away. His shoulders were broad and muscled. Auburn hair curled down his abdomen until it became a nest for the most masculine part of him. He was ready. His thighs and calves were well shaped and powerful. He was perfect in every way.

When he lay beside her, it was all she could do not to stroke and explore his body. Everything about his hard angles and dark shadows enticed her.

He undid the strings of her chemise and pantaloons, his tongue following his fingers. Delight caught her unawares and tossed her high. Contented sounds escaped her.

He chuckled deep in his chest. 'I wondered if you would purr.' He nuzzled her neck and then lower until his mouth took her breast. 'Now I know.'

He sucked and nipped. She made little gasping sounds.

Her hands circled him and her nails dug into his back. She was oblivious to everything but his mouth on her and where his fingers were going. They glided along her flesh, past her stomach and lower. She gasped in surprise when he first touched her. Her loins clenched pleasurably. His mouth returned to hers and the kiss he gave her was so deep she thought he would devour her.

Her nails raked his back as he gave her more pleasure than she had ever thought possible. When he broke from her lips, she whimpered and tried to force him back.

He laughed. 'No, sweetings. I want to watch you.'

She was beyond embarrassment. The things he

was doing to her created sensations that made her body spasm and twist.

He watched her face as his hands moved gently, but firmly against and in her flesh, dipping and stroking and exciting. She strained against him. It was too much.

'Open your legs,' he murmured, his voice so husky it was more a growl than words.

She opened slumberous eyes to see him poised above her. She did as she was told. He fit between her thighs as though he belonged there. She sighed with delight as he settled himself.

'Wrap your legs around me.'

Another order, but she was happy to do as he directed. He was hot and hard against her swollen flesh. She did not know what came next, but she moved her hips against his and felt the evidence of his desire.

He gathered her to him, kissing her deeply. Her breasts pressed like hot brands against his chest. He groaned and plunged into her.

Pain lashed Mary Margaret. Her eyes started open.

He stroked the hair from her face, his eyes catching hers. 'It is all right, sweetings. The pain will go away. I promise.'

For long minutes he did not move other than to kiss her gently and stroke her breasts and flanks.

She began to relax only to have her body start vibrating. He filled her to overflowing.

Slowly, he began to move. Sensations flowed over Mary Margaret with each thrust of his body. He stroked her and stoked her. A fire built in the pit of her loins. She felt tense beyond belief.

She shifted her hands to his hips and her nails dug into his flesh, urging him to greater speed and deeper penetration. With a groan, he obliged.

She twisted under him and pushed her hips higher. Whatever she sought was just over the next crest.

He pounded into her. She whimpered in need and pleasure—then exploded.

She gasped before a shout escaped her. His mouth fastened on hers and swallowed her sounds of release.

Seconds later, he groaned. His back arched and then he collapsed on her.

For long moments they lay, limbs tangled, breathing hard. When he finally rolled to her side, he pulled her to him. His hand cupped the back of her head and brought her to him for a tender kiss.

'Thank you,' he said softly.

She gazed at him, her body relaxed as never before. His eyes were slumberous, and his mouth was a sensual slash against his swarthy skin.

It came to her with a tiny shock that they had

made love. She was his mistress. She loved him. Had loved him forever, or she would never have been carried away by his lovemaking.

He smiled at her. 'Are you ready for more?'

Unable to speak for fear she would tell him everything, she only nodded. She did not think she could ever get enough of this closeness.

He moved over her, only this time she knew what to do.

Chapter Fourteen

Mary Margaret overslept the next morning. She woke with a start when Annabell landed on her bed with a plop.

'Wake up, sleepyhead. I had hot chocolate and toast brought up and you cannot eat them unless you are awake.'

Dazed and still feeling Ravensford's impassioned kisses on her skin, Mary Margaret finger-combed her hair back and stretched like a satisfied cat. 'What time is it?'

'Going on eleven.' Annabell smirked. 'You must have stayed up late after we returned.'

Surely Annabell did not know about her time in the Earl's chambers. She cast a surreptitious glance at the girl, but Annabell had moved on to the breakfast tray sitting on a nearby table. By now she knew Annabell well enough to realise that if the girl really had known something she would have stayed right where she was until she had got the information out of Mary Margaret. It was with a great deal of relief that she put on her robe and joined her charge at the table.

They poured chocolate and ate several slices of toast before Annabell said archly, 'Oh, I forgot to tell you. Mr Fox is below stairs, waiting to meet with you.'

Mary Margaret choked on a piece of crust. 'Thomas is here to see me and you forgot?'

Annabell laughed. 'Someone must put your brother-in-law in his proper place. I swear the man thinks he is some sort of Greek god and that all women should swoon at his feet.'

Mary Margaret goggled even as infinite relief flowed through her like water. She took a sip of chocolate. 'I thought you were rather taken with him.'

Annabell had the grace to look slightly uncomfortable, but only for a minute. 'Oh,' she said lightly, flipping her hand as though she tossed something away. 'I was only practising my skills at flirting. After all, being married and the clergy, he should be safe.'

'Prac—' Mary Margaret put her cup down before she spilled the contents on herself. 'That is abominable. A lady would never do such a thing.' Her laugh ameliorated her words.

Annabell smiled contentedly. 'A lady certainly would. What she would not do is admit it to anyone else unless she trusted that person implicitly.'

Mary Margaret sobered immediately. 'Thank you so much, Annabell. I cannot tell you how much that means to me.'

Annabell rose and dropped to her knees beside Mary Margaret and threw her arms around her. 'Oh, I shall miss you so when this Season is over. You have become like an older sister. The one I never had.' She hugged Mary Margaret tightly and kissed her on the cheek. 'I so wish you could stay part of Godmother's family or come to mine.' Her face lit up. 'That is it. I will beg Papa and Mama to let you come live with us. I have a younger sister who will need a chaperon. Unless I contract an acceptable alliance. Then you shall come stay with me.' She beamed with satisfaction.

Mary Margaret hugged Annabell back and fought off the tears her declaration had caused. 'My dear, that is so wonderful of you.' She carefully released the younger woman. 'But I could not live with you, your family or the Countess. Much as I would like to stay with you, I have a sister and niece who need me. I shall be returning to them when I leave here.'

'You cannot mean that.' Annabell jumped to her feet. 'Your sister is married to Mr Fox. The way he treats you he cannot want you with his family.'

Every word was true, but she could not, would not tell Annabell that. The girl did not need to know the sometimes ugly part of life. Instead she used Thomas as an excuse to end their conversation. She hugged Annabell and shooed her from the room. Minutes later she entered the drawing room where Thomas waited.

He whirled around at the sound of the door. 'It took you long enough.'

It took all of Mary Margaret's self-control not to cringe from the fury in Thomas's face. Annabell's little game of come-uppance would make this meeting nasty.

'I thought you would call tomorrow. I was asleep when I heard you were here. I am sorry it took so long.'

His words lashed out. 'See that it does not happen again.'

She nodded. How she wished she was braver and could make herself stand up to his tyranny. Somehow she managed to defy Ravensford all the time, but not Thomas.

The best she could do was ask, 'Why are you here?'

The smile he gave her was not pleasant. 'Have

you heard the latest *on-dit* making the rounds of
the *ton*?'

She shook her head, not liking this. He was going to tell her something awful. She could feel it.

'I thought not,' he said with satisfaction. 'You
probably have not heard of White's betting book
either, have you?'

Again she shook her head. She was having difficulty getting a deep breath and her fingers were
starting to shake. He was enjoying this too much.

'It is a book that the premier men in London
write bets in. Your name is not in it, but it men-
tions you.' He gloated. 'In fact, there is a bet on
how long it will take Ravensford to set you up in
your own establishment as his mistress. Everyone
knows he bought you an entire wardrobe.'

She swayed and would have fallen but for the
chair behind her. As it was, she hit the seat so hard
she nearly sent it over backward.

She was ruined. Last night had been nothing to
Ravensford but part of a bet.

Black spots swam before her eyes.

'An interesting bit of information, don't you
think?' Thomas asked cruelly.

She could not even nod. She could barely sit
upright. Her heart was slowly crumbling to pieces.

She stared at nothing. Last night had been magical and magic did not last. She knew that. But, oh, how she had wanted it to.

And did this really make any difference? Ravensford had offered her marriage—again. She had all but said yes. So what if he did not love her and was only doing it to prevent a scandal? The aristocracy did not wed for love. That was something else she knew. But she loved him.

She closed her eyes.

'What are you doing here?'

Ravensford's cold voice penetrated the haze of pain surrounding her. She had not heard him enter. She had even forgotten that Thomas was here. It was strange how her world had gone from the crystal clarity of love to the dull blur of a heart wound.

'I came to speak with my sister-in-law,' Thomas answered, his voice equally chill.

'She does not seem interested in what you have to say.'

'Oh, she was. Believe me, she was.'

Thomas's voice was slick as oil on water. Mary Margaret wanted to jump up and slap him for destroying all her dreams, however far-fetched they had been. He was the one who had put her in the position to meet Ravensford and he was the one who had told her the truth and ruined everything.

She opened her eyes and looked directly at her brother-in-law. 'Go away, Thomas.'

He looked at her as though she had grown a second head. She nearly giggled, but it was too much effort. She felt a mild sense of wonder at her bravery, quickly gone.

'I will see you tonight at the ball,' Thomas said with heavy meaning.

She ignored him. Her emotions were too battered. *Ravensford had never said he loved her.* She had been too caught up in the wonder of what they were doing and his promise to care for her and hers that she had not realised that at the time.

He came and kneeled in front or her. Taking both her hands in his, he asked, 'What did he do to make you look this way?'

'He told me about the bet.'

'Ahh.' He leaned back on his heels. 'It was stupid of me to think you would not hear about it, but I had hoped.'

'For all your knowledge of the *ton* and politics, you are not very well versed in human nature.'

He shrugged and stood. 'It does not make any difference.'

She rose and moved to the door. 'You are deluding yourself, Ravensford.'

She left before he could stop her. She needed privacy and time to sort through her feelings, time to become numb, and headed for the gazebo.

She sat quietly in the sylvan green. Roses

scented the air and a light breeze kept her from getting hot. She loved it here.

Love. What an overused word. She loved cherries. She loved roses. She loved this gazebo. Then what did she feel for Ravensford? She cared if he was happy or hurt or angry. He was the person she thought the most about and cared the most for. She liked the way he considered others and went out of his way to help them. She liked everything about him.

Well…maybe some things irritated her, but not enough to matter.

Yes, she *loved* him. Everything else was only a like.

But what to do? He did not love her. He desired her, lusted after her. That was physical while love was emotional and spiritual. A flush warmed her as memories of last night heated her body. Perhaps there was the physical in love as well.

Marrying him would solve all her problems. He had the money and power to protect Emily and Annie from Thomas. He could give them a good life. She would be with the only man she would ever love or want to love. She would have his children. But being married to him when he did not love her would be a bitter pill.

She jumped up and paced the tiny, enclosed space. She could become his mistress. He would still provide protection for Emily and Annie. She might still bear at least one of his children—a bastard.

She stopped and buried her face in her hands. She could not do that to any child of hers.

Nor would he want to marry her if he ever found out that Thomas had placed her with the Countess in order to steal from her. It would not matter that she never intended to carry out Thomas's plan. It would be enough that she had allowed herself to go along with Thomas. Ravensford would despise her if he ever learned that. She could not bear the thought of being married to him when he found out and seeing his contempt every time he looked at her.

If he loved her, truly loved her, he might forgive her.

No, it would be better to go to the Countess and ask for her salary. It would not provide what Ravensford would, but it would be better for all of them this way. That had always been her plan.

Her decision made, Mary Margaret wondered why she did not feel at least a little better. But she did not.

She found the Countess in her suite and waited patiently until the older woman would see her. She had plenty of time to marvel at her continued brav-

ery. In the past two hours, she had put herself forward more than she had in her entire life—except
when dealing with Ravensford. She pushed that
painful memory aside. There was no time to wal-
low in misery as the Countess's maid, Jane, had
just opened the door.

'Her ladyship will see you now.' She frowned
fiercely at Mary Margaret and barely moved
enough to allow the younger woman to get by.

'Thank you,' Mary Margaret said quietly.

Jane had never liked her. Having to pack her
clothes for the trip from Ireland had only made the
animosity worse.

'My lady.' Mary Margaret curtsied.

The Countess gave her a stony look. 'What do
you want?'

Not a good start, Mary Margaret thought, but
then there never was with this woman. It took all
her willpower not to wring her hands. That would
only give the Countess satisfaction.

'It is the end of the quarter.' Perhaps the woman
would take a hint.

'So?' She looked back at the embroidery in her
lap.

Mary Margaret was not surprised, but she was
angry. 'My salary is due.'

The Countess turned back to Mary Margaret, her
eyes hard as fine gems and her mouth a cruel line.

'Salary? You have no salary coming. It was all spent to replace my cape that you convinced my foolish son you needed.'

'What?' Mary Margaret felt as though she had taken a direct hit to the stomach. 'But I sent it back to you. It was in perfect shape. I made sure myself.'

The Countess made a tiny, derisive snort. 'Do you really think I would wear something after you had? And there are all the clothes Andrew purchased for you. You will be a long time repaying those.'

Worse and worse. Panic rose its ugly head, and it was all Mary Margaret could do to make herself breathe. This was beyond reasonable.

'Why are you doing this?' Her voice was a deep rasp of anguish. 'I have never done anything to you. All I have ever wanted was to be a good servant and companion.'

The Countess sneered, her lovely face marred by hate. 'You have seduced my only child. Do you think I don't know what has been going on? You blanch, as you should. You are no better than the sluts who ply their wares in Covent Garden.'

Mary Margaret felt light-headed and wondered if she would further disgrace herself by fainting. She swayed but managed to stay upright.

'I have done nothing of the kind,' she said, but even to her, her voice sounded weak and false.

He had seduced her. Surely that made a difference. Didn't it? Not to this woman. Not to anyone but her.

A sly look replaced the previous fury on the Countess's countenance. 'I want you out of this house immediately. I will provide you with money to return to Ireland. If you do this, I will forget about everything else. But do not ever come near my son again.'

Blow on blow. She could get back to Ireland, but once there would have nothing to live on, let alone provide for Emily and Annie.

The small rebellious and brave part of her that seemed to be growing by the hour wanted to defy the Countess. That part wanted to marry Ravensford and be damned to the consequences. It gave her courage now.

'I need more than passage home. I need money to live on.'

She trembled at her temerity. Just days or even hours ago she would not have been able to say those things. But it was done. She kept her gaze on the other woman instead of looking away as she longed to do.

The Countess drew herself up. 'You are a bold piece. How much do you want?'

'What is due me for this last quarter worked.'

'Done,' the Countess said. 'Now get out of my sight.'

Mary Margaret did so with alacrity. She rushed out of the room, the door slamming behind her, and right into Ravensford's arms.

'Where are you going in such a hurry?'

'Home.'

The word was out of her mouth before she had time to even think. Her nerves were jangling and her mind was numb.

His face showed no emotion. 'Ireland?'

She nodded.

'Because of my mother or because of the bet?' His voice was dangerously quiet, but Mary Margaret had been through too much in the last twenty-four hours to care.

'Both.'

'I think not,' he said softly, too softly.

Before she knew what was happening, he dragged her back into his mother's room. 'Out,' he ordered Jane who stood her ground until the Countess nodded.

'You have overstepped yourself this time, Mother,' he said.

She glared down her aristocratic nose at him even though she remained seated and he towered over her. 'I am only trying to protect you from your own folly. She is nothing but an adventuress. I should have never brought her into my household.'

Ravensford still held her so Mary Margaret could not flee. She had to listen to them discuss her as though she was not present. The tiny core of rebellion growing inside her flared to life.

'I am not an object for the two of you to bicker over.'

'Keep quiet,' the Countess ordered.

'I am a human being with feelings.'

The Countess gave her a contemptuous look. 'You are little better than—'

'Mother,' Ravensford said. 'I warn you. Mary Margaret is going to marry me. What you say to her now will impact on what happens to you after we are wed.'

The Countess paled, her translucent skin looking like a ghost. Her eyes were bright flames. 'I will not allow you to do such a thing, Andrew.'

Mary Margaret twisted in his hold, but he tightened his grip. 'I did not agree,' she said softly, wondering why even now she contradicted him.

Because she wanted to marry him for love. Nor would he want to marry her if he ever found out that she had been sent here to steal from his mother.

He gazed down at her. 'Oh, you agreed. You agreed very willingly.'

She saw the fire and hunger leap into his eyes and knew exactly what he meant. By giving herself to him last night, she had, in his mind, committed to him. He was right, she had at the time.

'Things have changed,' she said, her voice deep and raspy with remembered pain. 'For me.'

'But not for me.'

'Andrew.' The Countess's tone demanded attention. 'I won't have it. If you marry her, I will do everything in my power to see that she is ostracised by Society.'

Compassion softened the angles of his face. 'That does not matter, Mother. Not everyone cares about being accepted by the *ton*. I don't. I am sure Mary Margaret does not. And we all know that Lady Holland does not. Nor has her lack of acceptance impacted on Lord Holland's political career,' he ended with a meaningful look.

The Countess huffed. 'I was not about to suggest that Lady Holland's scandalous past has hurt Lord Holland in the least. But no decent woman will go to their house.'

Ravensford shook his head. 'I doubt it matters to them, Mother.'

'Well, it should. Just as it should matter to you.' She cast a venomous look at Mary Margaret. 'You will be sorry if you defy me. She won't make you happy.' Suddenly, like the sun peaking through clouds, a wistfulness entered her eyes. 'Not like your father and I were.'

'She is right,' Mary Margaret said. 'Ours would be a marriage of convenience. You would grow tired of me.'

A strange light turned his eyes a deeper green. 'I am going to announce our engagement tonight during the ball.'

Both women gasped.

'No,' the Countess ordered.

'You cannot,' Mary Margaret whispered, horrified.

'I can and I will.'

Chapter Fifteen

Ravensford turned from the fire in time to see Mary Margaret framed in the drawing-room doorway. Fierce pride filled him.

After him, she was the first one down. Jones bowed himself out, leaving the two of them alone.

Madame Bertrice's gown accomplished everything he had wished for. The deep pink brought colour to her face, giving her the famous cream-and-roses complexion. Her tilted eyes glowed like green brilliants. Even the demure, almost harsh, line of her chignon appeared elegant, as though it had been specially designed to show off the gown's plunging neckline.

Mary Margaret's bosom swelled above the fine silk, drawing his eye to the dark valley that he longed to explore. Once had not been enough. He was not sure a lifetime would be enough. From the first moment he had heard the sultry purr of her voice he had desired her. Tonight she was his. Or would be, he thought ironically, seeing the coldness in her face, once he had convinced her that marriage was best.

'You are beautiful,' he said. He picked the jewellery box up from the table beside him and opened it. 'These will complement your dress.' He took out the grey pearls.

Her gaze flicked to the necklace and back to him. 'They are not appropriate.'

There was no bending in her. 'You have gained strength since I first met you.'

'I have had to.' Her voice was lightly tinged with bitterness. 'Is your mother down?' Only now did her tone hold a hint of discomfort.

'My mother has nothing to do with this, Mary Margaret.' When she did not respond, he added, 'She will be going back to Ireland soon. You and I will stay here. Your sister and niece are being brought here.'

Mary Margaret listened to his words and wondered why he was doing all these things. He did not love her, yet he would not let her go.

After leaving his mother's suites earlier, he had told her that no matter what the Countess had said or offered to pay her, she was not leaving. Since that time, she had been a virtual prisoner in the house. The only thing that had brought her down for the evening was his vow that he had already sent for her sister. She owed him her presence that he seemed so insistent on having.

'I will not marry you,' she said yet again. 'Your mother is right.'

But how she longed to do so. If he only loved her she would take the risk. Even now, it hurt just to tell him no when she wanted so badly to tell him yes. But it would take more than lust for him to tolerate her if he ever found out that she had been sent by Thomas to rob his mother and she had not told Thomas no.

'Turn around,' he said, more gently. 'I am determined that you will wear these.'

She sighed. How much longer could she keep fighting him? She did not know. For the moment it was easier to acquiesce. After all, he had already bought her an entire wardrobe, and although she did not wear any of the clothes, the entire world knew about them. They were still packed in boxes in her room. She turned.

His fingers brushed the nape of her neck and his warm breath fanned her skin. She clenched her hands into fists to keep from turning and wrapping them into his hair. He made her blood sing and her heart thrill.

'Please hurry,' she rasped.

'Am I bothering you?' His voice was as rich as cream and as potent as the liquor he drank.

'No.'

He chuckled low in his throat. 'I'm almost done. Then there are the ear bobs and the bracelets.'

She nearly groaned. This was torture, and drat the man, he knew it. No matter how she tried, her body and soul responded to him. No matter how she strove to hide her reaction he knew.

His hands shifted to her shoulders and he turned her unresisting body so that she faced him. 'Say yes.'

She caught back a moan. How she wanted to accept him. She wanted that more than anything. If only she could. If only they could somehow make it work. If only he loved her then she would take the chance. Romantic fool that she was, she believed that love could make anything work.

She knew he watched her but she studiously looked away. The last thing she wanted was to see the hunger in his eyes that he did nothing to hide. She wanted his love, not just his passion. He didn't love her and, foolish woman that she was, she wanted love.

'I cannot,' she whispered. 'I must not. Believe me, this is for the best.'

'Then look at me when you refuse and convince me that you speak the truth.' Anger tinged his words now and his eyes, when she looked back at him, flared.

Before she could say anything, and she did not know what to say, the door opened and Jones announced, 'The Countess of Ravensford and Miss Winston. Mr Fox.'

Mary Margaret broke from Ravensford's hold. The expression on the Countess's face as she watched them made Mary Margaret feel as though she had been caught doing something despicable. In the Countess's opinion, she had.

Thomas subjected her to a narrowed scrutiny. 'Cosy, aren't we,' he said sarcastically.

She arched one brow. 'I thought you were not invited until after dinner?' It was a low hit, but it gave her satisfaction.

He smirked. 'Your delightful charge invited me. I considered her wishes to take precedence over Ravensford's.'

Annabell came up to them and beamed. 'I see you two have finally worked everything out. I am so glad.' She hugged Mary Margaret. 'It will be wonderful having you in the family.'

Mary Margaret returned the girl's hug. 'You are so impetuous, Annabell,' she chided gently. 'The Earl and I have no agreement and nothing to arrange.'

Annabell stepped back and gave the two of them

an arch look. 'I did not fall off the turnip wagon yesterday.' She laughed and moved away.

It was just as well. Jones announced more arrivals. Dinner would consume the near future. Then the ball. Mary Margaret knew the entire evening would be a crush of bodies.

And she still had to tell Thomas that she was not going to steal the Countess's jewellery tonight. Discomfort was a condition she was becoming depressingly familiar with.

'Nice pearls,' Thomas hissed. 'Make sure you take them with you.'

She jumped, not having heard him come up behind her. 'Be careful. Someone could overhear.'

He laughed. It was not a pleasant sound. She moved quickly away only to find herself caught up by Ravensford. Before she knew what he was doing, she was being introduced to everyone.

Ravensford smiled at each person as he presented her, but his eyes were hard chips until the introduction was graciously accepted. Mary Margaret realised that he was trying to present her to his Society and force them to accept her regardless of the rumours flying.

After an eternity, they went into dinner. Mary Margaret nearly fled the room when she realised she was to be seated beside Ravensford. Everyone looked at her and she did her best not to blush.

The only saving grace with the arrangement was that the Countess was at the opposite end of the table.

The woman across the table eyed Mary Margaret through her lorgnette. 'Where did you say you are from, Miss O'Brien?'

'Ireland, my lady.' Old habits die hard and it was not until the form of address was out that Mary Margaret realised it was inappropriate for her current situation.

'She is from Cashel, Ireland, Lady Steele,' Ravensford cut in. 'Near my mother's estate.' He gave the woman a feral smile. 'Would you care for more turtle soup?'

'Please,' Lady Steele said, turning her attention to the gentleman on her left.

Mary Margaret's dinner partner to her right, Mr Atworthy, asked, 'How long will you be staying in Town, Miss O'Brien?'

'Quite some time,' Ravensford said smoothly before she could answer.

Mr Atworthy looked from her to the Earl, his interest obviously piqued. 'Really? Are you by any chance Miss Winston's chaperon, Miss O'Brien?'

A direct question with only one answer. 'Yes,' she said firmly before Ravensford could reply.

She was grateful that her voice had not wavered. They would dine on her like a shark on a minnow if she faltered. Ravensford gave her an approving smile.

'She was, Atworthy. No more.'

Atworthy raised one brow. 'How intriguing.'

The next course arrived and while the bowls and plates were removed Mary Margaret tried to marshal her thoughts. If she could get through dinner, she could escape while everyone was going to the ballroom and the rest of the guests were arriving. She just had to grit her teeth and bear the next hour or so.

She was nearly ready to plead sickness when the Countess stood, indicating that the ladies were to withdraw. She stood with alacrity even though she knew she had to wait for the other women to precede her from the room. All the gentlemen's gazes turned to her, watching as though she were an exotic animal and they did not know what she might do next.

A month ago she would have done her best to pretend they were not there. Even an hour ago she would have done so. But now she was tired and irritable. With a courage she had never thought she possessed, she stared each man down. The only one who refused to look away was Perth. He silently toasted her with the last of his dinner wine.

She finally swept from the room, buoyed up by Perth's silent support. Her joy was short-lived.

Two women she had previously met stood together, heads close. The first sniffed haughtily. 'So that is Ravensford's lightskirt. She isn't much. However, he has gone too far introducing her to polite society. I, for one, will never invite her anywhere.'

There it was. Even if she let herself weaken and marry Ravensford, it would be miserable. Not that she cared what the old biddy thought, but despite his earlier words, Ravensford might. And what would he and they think if they knew about Thomas's plan? It did not bear dwelling on.

Rather than continue to subject herself to such treatment, Mary Margaret decided it was time to go to her room. Later, after the dancing had started, she would come back down and seek out Thomas.

With weary relief, she entered her room and closed the door behind her. She would lie down for a few minutes and try to regain her strength.

She set the candle on the table and snuffed the flame. She stretched out on her bed with a weary sigh, careful to smooth her dress so as not to wrinkle it any more than necessary. The last thing she wanted was to get a maid to help her undress and then dress again.

Mary Margaret woke with a start. The room was too dark to see anything clearly, but she sensed she was not alone.

She sat up and swung her legs over the side of the bed until her feet touched the floor. 'Who is there?' she asked in a voice that just kept from trembling.

'Not Ravensford,' Thomas said nastily.

A kind of relief slumped her shoulders. Thomas was not someone she wanted in her bedchamber, but he would not hurt her. Or had not done so yet.

She lit the candle by the bed and carried it over to the chair beside Thomas. She sat down and placed the candle on the table.

'Why are you here?'

He snorted in disgust. 'Don't be any more stupid than you have to be. Why do you think I am here? Where are the jewels?'

The single light threw his handsome face into harsh relief. His eyes were dark sockets. Mary Margaret found that she was suddenly tense. Still, there was no sense in prolonging the inevitable.

She licked dry lips. 'I assume they are in the Countess's room. Or the Earl's safe.'

'When do you intend to get them?' he asked softly, his voice silky smooth.

She decided to get closer to the door. She stood and walked casually away, hoping he would think she was moving from nervousness caused by contemplating the theft.

'Where do you think you are going?'

He moved too fast. She broke for the door. He caught her, his fingers gripping her wrist cruelly.

'I asked you a question,' he said, tightening his hold.

Her heart beat like a drum. It was all she could do to keep herself from shouting for help. She told herself she was being silly. He might be hurting her, but still this was only Thomas. He could not reach Emily and Annie. He had no hold over her.

She took a deep breath and stared up at him. She was barely able to make out his features, but she sensed he was tense.

'I was leaving…but not to get the jewels.' She twisted her arm in a vain attempt to get free. 'I am not going to steal from the Countess.'

He tossed her against the wall. The force of contact knocked the air out of her lungs. She gasped.

'Tell me that again,' he threatened.

She forced herself to straighten up even though her chest hurt badly. She told herself she knew he would not seriously injure her, but she still feared the pain he could cause.

'Who's in there?' Ravensford's voice said from outside.

Relief flooded Mary Margaret only to be followed by dread. He would keep Thomas from doing anything more to her, but she had no doubt that Thomas would see that she paid for refusing to help him. She sighed and slumped against the wall.

'Come in,' Thomas said.

Ravensford entered and closed the door behind himself. He carried a candelabra with five candles. Light radiated out in a circle, so bright it hurt Mary Margaret's eyes after the dimness of seconds before.

'What are you doing here?' Ravensford's baritone was deep and dangerous.

Thomas smirked. 'Perhaps you should ask your *chère amie*.' He gave Mary Margaret a sly look. 'Or have you already told him?'

She knew she looked guilty when Thomas laughed.

'No, you have not.' Contempt dripped from every word. 'I swear you have no spine. Just like your sister. You sleep with the man but cannot find the courage to tell him the truth about why you are working for his mother.'

Shame burned through Mary Margaret. Thomas was a cad, but he said only the truth right now.

She could not make herself look at Ravensford. She looked at a spot near his shoulder. She did not want to see the disgust on his face when she told him. She could not stand to see his eyes fill with the same contempt that shone in Thomas's.

'Tell him,' Thomas said, 'or I will.'

She cast her brother-in-law a venomous look.

'I was supposed to steal your mother's jewellery tonight. That is why Thomas is here, to pick up the gems.'

There. The awful truth was out. It was over. Now he would hate her. He would be thankful she had refused his offer of marriage. He would throw her out when he threw out Thomas.

A single tear escaped her control. Not only would she never see him again, but he would always remember her this way—as a thief and cheat and coward.

Pain such as she had never imagined possible welled up inside her. So much pain, quickly followed by anger—at herself, at Thomas.

Without thinking, propelled by the mingled pain and anger, she launched herself at Thomas's sneering face. She balled her fist and let loose. She connected and Thomas rocked back on his heels.

She glared at him. 'I hate you for what you are and what you have done to my sister and what you tried to make me do.' Tears started down her cheeks in earnest and she twisted away from his shocked face. 'But most of all I hate myself for not being strong enough to tell you no right from the start.'

She heard scuffling and the heavy thud of someone hitting the floor. Thomas sprawled on the rug, one hand on his red jaw. Ravensford towered over him.

'Get up and get out. Leave England if you know what is good for you. Don't return to Ireland. With Mary Margaret's confession I can have the magistrate waiting for you there. Once word is out about what you planned, you will be ruined. No one wants a curate like you. And don't try to find your wife and daughter. If I catch you near them, I will have you horsewhipped like the cur you are.'

Shivers raced up Mary Margaret's spine. She hoped never to see Ravensford this deadly angry again. Her heart twisted. She did not have to worry. She would never see him again at all.

Thomas turned bitter eyes on Mary Margaret. 'Don't worry about your precious sister. I never wanted her. She got pregnant and I had to marry her because of my position. All I ever wanted in life was what I deserved, what I was born to. Your refusal to steal has only delayed that. I'll find someone else with more guts than a worm.'

He strode away, pausing inches from Ravensford. 'She's not worth whatever she will cost you.

Nor is her mealy-mouthed sister. You are welcome
to the lot.'

Anger burned away Mary Margaret's tears.
'How dare you? How dare you speak of them like
that? If Emily was pregnant before you wed, it was
because you seduced her and she loved you too
much to say no. You are despicable.'

'Get out now,' Ravensford said, 'before I thrash
you to within an inch of your life.'

Thomas left without another word. Silence filled
the room like dirt in a grave. Mary Margaret felt
like her life was finished. From now on she would
merely exist. But at least Emily was free of
Thomas.

'Mary Margaret,' Ravensford said softly, 'come
here. Please.'

She looked at him, expecting to see contempt or
dislike and instead saw compassion and another
emotion she did not dare name. 'I think it would
be better if I left now.'

He shook his head. 'What have I been saying to
you all this time?'

She stood mute. There was nothing left she
could say. He knew everything about her and she
knew he could not still want to marry her. He had
not wanted to marry her in the first place. Only his
honour had made him propose.

'Mary Margaret, if I have to come and get you I will make sure you don't get away.'

'Why?' Agony twisted her soul. 'You don't want me. You never wanted me—except in your bed. Then when the bet was made you were too much the gentleman not to propose.' She gulped air, trying to ease some of the tension tearing her apart. 'Please, Ravensford, don't do this. I can be gone immediately. You have done enough just by getting Thomas out of my sister's life. And I thank you from my heart.'

A tiny smile tugged at his mouth. 'I don't want your thanks from the heart, Mary Margaret.' He moved slowly toward her. 'I want more than that.'

She tilted back her head to see his face. His eyes were dark, his cheeks sharp lines. If she did not know it was impossible, she would say he wanted her—still.

'I have given you everything I have,' she whispered.

He stopped when only inches separated them. 'Have you?' A fierce predatory gleam lit his face. 'Then tell me.'

'Don't do this,' she pleaded. 'It is not fair that I love you and you don't feel the same about me.' She buried her face in her hands. 'There, I have told you. Once more I was not strong enough to walk from here without doing as you bid.'

With exultation he grabbed her and cradled her against his chest. One hand angled her reluctant head up so that he looked down at her. The other hand burrowed into her thick hair.

'Foolish, love. You are the strongest woman I know. You have cared for your sister, worked for my mother and stood up to Fox—not to mention me.'

Love. He had called her love.

Hope flared, only to die. 'I am weak or I would have never agreed to Thomas's plan.'

He kissed her gently. 'You had no choice. I heard him threaten you that day in my mother's library.'

'What?' She went rigid, both hands pressing against his chest in an effort to get free. He held her closer. 'You have known all along?'

He nodded. 'I knew you did not want to do as he said, but that you feared for Emily. Later I learned Emily is your sister.'

'But why did you let the charade go on? Why have you treated me so well?' Confusion now held her still in his embrace. She did not know what to think.

He grinned ruefully. 'I was intrigued by you, by everything about you.' He stroked one finger down her jaw to her chin where the cleft was. 'I still am. I think I always will be.'

'But I am nothing.'

'Stop that.' He shook her. 'You are kind and caring. You were willing to do anything to help your sister. And Annabell adores you. The servants like and respect you.'

She was dazed. 'But you don't love me. You cannot. We are from different worlds and I have lived a lie in your home.' Every word hurt, but they had to be said. 'And I want love when I marry.'

'Ah, Mary Margaret.' He stroked her hair back from her face. 'Have I been so good at hiding my feelings? Don't you know that I love you? Can't you sense it when I touch you, when I kiss you? And when we made love, didn't you feel me worship you with my body?'

Stunned, she would have slid to the floor if he had not been holding her. 'I know you desire me. But that is not love.'

'You have so much to learn about men, my love. Making love to you is a form of loving you. Just as caring for you and caring for your sister. Men show their love through deeds, not through words.' He paused as though gathering his courage. 'Mary Margaret, I love you. I want to marry you.'

Hope began to fill her heart. Perhaps there was a chance for them. Perhaps he truly did love her.

She tried her last argument. 'What about your mother?'

'She can go to Ireland or she can accept you and stay around and watch our children grow.' He gazed lovingly at her. 'Because now that I have found you and made you admit that you love me, I am not letting you get away.'

The hope that had started filled her to overflowing. She could no longer refuse him or herself. She loved him too much to let him go now.

'Then we will have to make this work.'

'Yes, my love, we will.'

Epilogue

One year later…

Mary Margaret stood in the doorway to the nursery and silently watched her mother-in-law. The Countess held the future Earl of Ravensford, cooing at the infant like the besotted grandmother she was.

A large, warm hand twined around hers and pulled her away. Ravensford, her husband, smiled down at her as he guided her along the hall.

'My mother will take good care of our son, sweetings.'

She snuggled into his side. 'I know. I just like to watch the two of them together. It reassures me that there is a gentle, caring side to your mother.'

He tenderly smoothed a strand of hair from her

brow. 'I know she still is not always nice to you. I am sorry for that. More than I can say.'

She went on tiptoe and kissed him lightly. 'I know. Things are better and with time—who knows? She and I might become bosom friends.'

He shook his head in wonder. 'Your continual ability to look at the positive always amazes me.'

He caught her lips with his, deepening the kiss until she leaned against his chest in complete surrender. He was her entire world.

'Aunt,' a young, feminine voice said in shocked tones. 'You and Uncle Andrew are going to scandalise the servants.'

Another woman's warm laugh filled the area. 'Annie, leave your aunt and uncle alone. Theirs is a love match.'

Mary Margaret grinned at her niece and sister. 'I am so glad you decided to come stay with us.'

'As am I,' Ravensford seconded. 'Not only do you provide additional family for my love, but you are safer from Fox if he should decide my threat is hollow.'

All three females gazed adoringly at him, but his wife hugged him. 'Thomas would never doubt you. He ran from my room that night like a fox fleeing the hounds.'

'And just what was he doing in your room?' the Countess demanded, having come up on the group without their noticing. Baby Andrew cooed contentedly in his grandmother's arms.

Mary Margaret reached for her son. 'It is time for his feeding,' she murmured, having decided to nurse her child instead of having a wet-nurse. She cast a mischievous glance at her husband as she left him to deal with his mother.

But Ravensford was not going to be deserted. 'Excuse me, ladies. I will explain everything to you later, Mother. Right now a father's place is with his wife and son.'

Mary Margaret chuckled as she sat down in the rocker and put her baby to her breast. Baby Andrew had just settled in when Ravensford closed the nursery door. He looked at his wife and child, the boy's mouth sucking avidly at one milky-white breast.

'Your bosom is larger than before,' Ravensford murmured, taking a seat beside them.

She intended to only glance at him, but the desire he made no effort to hide caught her. A flush mounted her skin, starting where her child suckled and rising to her cheeks.

'Ravensford,' she murmured in slight protest. 'This is not the time.'

'I know,' he muttered, his voice a husk. 'But after our son has his fill I insist on having mine.

He needs a little sister and I've a mind to do my best to provide him with one.'

Excitement curled in Mary Margaret's stomach. 'And I've a mind to help you, my lord.'

Ravensford leaned over and kissed her. 'I love you.'

'And I you,' she replied, meaning it with all her heart and soul.

* * * * *

Modern Romance™
...seduction and
passion guaranteed

Tender Romance™
...love affairs that
last a lifetime

Sensual Romance™
...sassy, sexy and
seductive

Sizzling Romance™
...sultry days and
steamy nights

Medical Romance™
...medical drama on
the pulse

Historical Romance™
...rich, vivid and
passionate

29 new titles every month.

*With all kinds of Romance for
every kind of mood...*

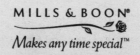

MILLS & BOON®

Makes any time special™

MAT3

MILLS & BOON®

Historical Romance™

AN HONOURABLE THIEF by Anne Gracie

Hugo Devenish couldn't explain why he suspected
the innocent-looking Miss Kit Singleton of the spate of
robberies that coincided with her arrival in London.
When clues started adding up, he resolved to make
her stop playing such a dangerous game. But Kit
needed to fulfil the pledge she made to her dying
father – and she couldn't confide in anyone, not even
the man with whom she was falling in love…

Regency

A MOST UNSEEMLY SUMMER by Juliet Landon

Reign of Elizabeth I…intrigue, treachery and passion…

Having learnt how to protect and care for herself,
Lady Felice Marwelle is the obvious choice to oversee
the final renovations to her family's new home. To her
dismay, the surveyor of the project, Sir Leon Gascelin,
feels he must appoint himself as guardian of this
capable and determined woman. Is it to stop tongues
wagging about their co-habitation, as he claims? Or
has Felice been sent to this dangerously attractive man
to be well and truly tamed?

On sale 5th October 2001

FREE

2 BOOKS
AND A SURPRISE GIFT!

We would like to take this opportunity to thank you for reading this Mills & Boon® book by offering you the chance to take TWO more specially selected titles from the Historical Romance™ series absolutely FREE! We're also making this offer to introduce you to the benefits of the Reader Service™—

★ FREE home delivery
★ FREE monthly Newsletter
★ FREE gifts and competitions
★ Exclusive Reader Service discounts
★ Books available before they're in the shops

Accepting these FREE books and gift places you under no obligation to buy; you may cancel at any time, even after receiving your free shipment. Simply complete your details below and return the entire page to the address below. *You don't even need a stamp!*

YES! Please send me 2 free Historical Romance books and a surprise gift. I understand that unless you hear from me, I will receive 4 superb new titles every month for just £2.99 each, postage and packing free. I am under no obligation to purchase any books and may cancel my subscription at any time. The free books and gift will be mine to keep in any case.

H1ZEC

Ms/Mrs/Miss/Mr ....Initials ....
BLOCK CAPITALS PLEASE

Surname ....

Address ....

....

....Postcode ....

Send this whole page to:
UK: FREEPOST CN81, Croydon, CR9 3WZ
EIRE: PO Box 4546, Kilcock, County Kildare (stamp required)